WHEN I WAS YOUR GIRLFRIEND

NIKKI HARMON

WHEN I WAS YOUR GIRLFRIEND

NIKKI HARMON

All characters in this publication are fictitious, and any resemblance to real persons, living or dead, is purely coincidental.

WHEN I WAS YOUR GIRLFRIEND
Copyright © 2015 Nikki Harmon

Dedicated to

Kelly

✻ CHAPTER ONE ✻

As I pull up in front of the office, I see they are already there, hopping around, snuggling, rubbing noses, and laughing at their private jokes. I love them. I hate them. It's complicated. Leslie and Laurie are seemingly the perfect couple. They are smart, good-looking, employed, and deeply in love. Together for four years, they are three months pregnant and they sought me out to be their midwife.

Of course they did. We could all be best friends and maybe we will be after the baby is born. I am the only black lesbian midwife in the Philadelphia area. Mt. Airy Midwives brought me in as soon as I got my CNM degree from Georgetown University. One of five midwives with two OBs on staff, we stay fairly busy. This is a great area of the city to work—full of conscientious, middle-income, well-educated families. I smile at the couple, park my hybrid (I am also conscientious, middle-income, and well-educated) and climb out trying to look composed and not spill my coffee.

"Hi guys! I hope you haven't been waiting long. Let me just get my keys …"

Laurie, the pregnant one, takes two steps back. "The smell of coffee still gets to me," she says.

Leslie steps forward to help with my bags. She is that warm cocoa brown color, just ever so slightly butch, like maybe she just has a hint of biceps under that tailored blouse. But it's her voice, a voice you could sink into like a warm bath. Her laugh is deep and hearty like a woman full of confidence and love. If she wasn't married and I wasn't a professional … ah well. I thank her and give her my heaviest bag, which she swings over her shoulder with ease.

Looking past her, I see our receptionist, Tracy Ann, strolling up the street jingling her huge ring of keys as though she has all the time in the world. Seeing my look, she shifts into a trot and puffs up to us.

"Oh, hi! I didn't realize there was an early appointment today. I'm so sorry. Little Larry was such a handful today, threw all his Cheerios on the floor."

As she prattles on and opens the door, we all file inside and try to get ourselves situated. I rush to my office, turn on the heater, and get ready for "The Perfect Couple." Uh oh, I hope I'm not getting bitter. The heater is for the comfort of my half-clothed patients. I love the briskness of this time of year. It's still chilly, but the hint of spring is there. The morning light is warmer, softer. If I squint, I can see round scarlet buds on the trees outside my office window. Spring is coming and that makes me happy.

Laurie comes in first. She is one of those women who, though over 30 years old, could still be described as adorable. She has round dimpled cheeks, she never stops smiling, and she gives enormous, totally uncalled for long, hard hugs like it could be the last time she ever sees you.

"Dee! Oh, my gosh, I'm still so excited to finally be pregnant!" She giggles and reaches to engulf me. Leslie comes in next. I see a camera in her hand.

"We need a picture of you for our pregnancy album!" I smile and put on my stethoscope. Click!

After a successful visit, baby is fine, Laurie is fine, and Leslie is nervous but fine. I sit back and put on some Erykah Badu. I put a note in Laurie's chart and check my schedule. I have 30 minutes until my next appointment. I retrieve and finish my tepid coffee. I know it's corny, but I love my job. Since I was 12 and found out how babies were born, I've always wanted to deliver babies. I thought it would be the coolest thing in the world to assist with bringing life onto the planet, into a family. Who knows whom that baby will grow up to be—another Einstein or Dickinson or Ghandi, an inventor, a peacemaker, or just a really good person. Of course, I have no control over the babies. But I love taking care of pregnant women the way they should be taken care of, and bringing their babies into the world with love and patience. It's one of those things that is absolutely mundane and absolutely miraculous all at the same time.

In college, I almost changed my mind. I got political and decided that I should try to help people who really needed help—poor people, oppressed people, disenfranchised people. I decided I wanted to go and work in South America and help dig wells for clean drinking water for the villagers there. I told my mom my idea during a Christmas break.

"Mmmm hmmm. That's nice, dear," she said.

The next day I happened upon my student loan statement casually sitting out on the dining room table. Forty-five thousand dollars and I was just a junior. The following day I noticed a newspaper article about college students moving back home with their parents because they couldn't afford to live anywhere else. By the end of the month, random relatives casually forwarded emails about the low efficacy rates of non-profit organizations, the dangers of working in the jungle—gangs, militia, disease, etc.

The day I was leaving to go back to school, my mom suggested we stop at Fran's Used Book Store to see if we could find anything interesting. Somehow I stumbled upon *Spiritual Midwifery* by Ina May Gaskin, the classic midwifery book, and picked it up for three dollars. My mom drove me to 30th Street Station, hugged me goodbye, re-wrapped my scarf, pulled down my hat, tucked $20 in my pocket and drove away with a smile on her face. By the time I was back in New Haven, I was re-thinking my South American adventure. Mom is no fool.

I hear a knock at the door, quickly turn down the music, and glance at my daily schedule. It's time for Beth and Josh. A sweet couple, in their second trimester, I can't wait to see how they're doing.

Seven hours later, my day is over. None of my patients are in active labor or anywhere near it. I'm not on-call until the weekend and my evening is wide open. Despite being done for the day, I hang around to chat with Meadow, one of my fellow midwives. We're like family and it's been a while since we've caught up.

Meadow looks exactly as you would imagine, probably because her parents waited until she was six months old to name her. You can do that kind of stuff on a commune. She has sandy blond, curly hair, occasionally tied back with yarn or ribbon. Of course she has freckles and widely spaced green eyes, a perfect hippie child who took the lifestyle to heart. But don't think she's soft or stupid. She's one of the smartest people I know. Insightful and intuitive, she can read me like a book.

"So Dee, why are you still here?" she asks. "It's a beautiful day. I figured you might have something fun planned for you and Pepper."

I cringe. Right, Pepper. Let me say right now that I hate her name. I do. It sounds stupid. No, not stupid, ridiculous.

However, I am an open-minded woman. How could I justify not dating someone just because her parents had no common sense and gave their daughter a stripper's name or a dog's name? Can't blame the child right?

We met at Marlene's, the only lesbian club in Philly. It was dark, I was slightly drunk, and she was so sexy and funny. "Pepper" sounded good at the club. It sounded good that night, all night long, it even sounded good the next morning. I had Pepper with my eggs. Oh, it was all good until I had to introduce her to my friends a few weeks later, then, not so good. They made jokes, of course, and then I got defensive.

Now I've been dating her for six months. In lesbian terms, that's almost married. I like her, but I don't love her even though I told her I did. She's a good woman. Smart, fun, kind, and she has a plan for her life. But for some reason, I just don't see myself with her. I know this. I've known it for five and a half months. As if on cue, my iPhone rings. It's Pepper, of course.

"Hey babe! We're having dinner downtown tonight with my friends then heading over to the club, OK? Can you pick me up by 7 p.m.? Wear something hot!... It's karaoke night."

Pepper is 26, only five years younger than me. But sometimes it makes a big difference. It's not the evening I had in mind, but I agree to it. I smirk at Meadow as she greets her patient, wave good-bye at Tracy Ann, and head on home.

CHAPTER TWO

After trying on my fifth outfit, I go back to my first choice, club jeans that make my butt look cute, and a white button-down shirt with a black tank underneath. I believe this is universally understood to be the never fail, lesbian going out look. In the summer, it could just be a white t-shirt. Back in the eighties, it was all about a black t-shirt, but times have changed and laundry detergent has gotten better.

I check myself out in the mirror. Do I still look as hot as I did in my twenties? (I know it wasn't that long ago but 31 has hit me hard!) Hmmm, maybe I'll add a touch of lipstick. Nah, maybe just some gloss. Fluff the hair, make sure the afro-curl thing is curling just right. It takes work making effortless look effortless. Twist here, tuck there, pat it all in place, do a practice dance to make sure my jeans still stretch, and I'm ready to go.

It takes me 15 minutes to get to Pepper's place. I plan to wait in the car, but three cell phone calls later, I reluctantly climb out and go to wait in her house. I'm not early; she is late, as usual. I know we as a people are not the most punctual bunch, but there is a time when it just gets downright inconsiderate and disrespectful.

I go in fussing and sighing about how she is always making me wait. She stops tweaking her hair in the mirror and walks over to me smiling. She kisses on my neck slowly, softly, giving me chills, she coos in my ear about how she thought about me all day, and then we kiss. It's fifteen minutes of making out that make me forget about all about my earlier indignation. I happily let myself be manipulated – literally and figuratively – and by the time she slides her hand out of my jeans and I slide myself out of the corner of her living room, I'm starving and content. I think I purred. Now I'm really hungry. Her cell is blowing up – her friends are feeling the inconsideration. I wonder briefly how she keeps them complacent.

By the time we make it to the restaurant, everybody exchanges knowing glances, nudging elbows and somehow it's assumed that our lateness was my doing—whatever! At least they ordered the food already. While she chats with her friends, I eat and listen. I watch her in her element and wonder how I fit in here. I think I catch them looking at me too, wondering the same thing. Pepper is beautiful to behold—not classically so, but her energy is contagious and she dominates the conversation. Like the bright red scarf draping over her shoulders that keeps drawing my eye, the conversation always turns back to her. She is the punctuation to every sentence and the motivation for each new topic. Her hair is cut extremely close to her head, almost a baldy but just a smidge shy of radical. But it's her eyes, those smoky, slanted, I'm-always-thinking-about-sex eyes. I think that's what keeps all of us hanging on her every word. It's like she's just about to start talking dirty any minute now.

"So, I just enrolled in a graduate program. I have to get back to school to get the lifestyle I deserve! You know what I'm saying?!?" she says.

Oh, she could be talking about a new apartment, car, or jewelry. Her eyes say she's talking about a trip to Victoria's Secret or the sex shop. It's the eyes.

We finish up our meal, pay the tab, and head out to Marlene's on 13th Street. It's a short walk, but the air is still cold in March. The conversation is lost in puffs of breath and clacking of heels on concrete. Nodding and smiling at the butchy bouncer at the door, we flash IDs and head straight for the bar with the best view of the little stage. It's Wednesday night, the unofficial "black women" night at the bar. Even amongst lesbians, there are cultural differences and they matter when you are hanging out with your friends. One cannot underestimate the importance of music when going to a club. If the music is irritating or boring, you are not going to have a good time and buy lots of drinks. So the owners of Marlene's have designated Wednesdays as Urban Night – R & B Karaoke early on and rap and hip-hop for the baby dykes with no jobs who can stay out til 2 a.m. on a weeknight. We take our seats, order our drinks, Jack and Coke for me, while Pepper starts scanning the sheet for what she will sing. I will not be singing. I cannot sing, not at all, not even one little bit. Trust me, I've tried.

"Pep," I ask, "why don't you do Natalie Cole? You have the voice and she's one of my favorite singers." Pepper looks at me like I'm crazy.

"I'm singing Rihanna. You know she's my favorite singer." I pout and stick my lip out. "Please, how about "This Will Be"?

"No," she says, "No-ella, ella, ella."

She cracks herself up, takes a sip of her Manhattan, and kisses my cheek. I reach around to hug her and look into those eyes. We kiss. She's really quite intoxicating.

As Pepper pulls gently away to get back to her friends and her list, I see something out the front door of the club. It's two young girls. They look like high school girls. One is waving an ID; the other is cowering behind looking as frightened as a rabbit. She is tugging on her friend's hand, but the bold girl is really trying to argue her way in. I admire her tenacity. The bouncer is not having it, not on black night! The girl finally gives up and walks away. Her friend looks relieved and they fade away into the night. I take a sip of my drink and think back to my first time at a gay club. It was not pretty.

⚜

It was my senior year in high school, early spring like now, and my best friend, Vivian Dupree, and I were venturing downtown one Saturday afternoon. There wasn't much for teenagers to do on the weekends in Philly. But we walked up and down South Street, bought some wristbands at Zipperhead, had some cheese fries at Ishkabibbles, and eventually got bored despite the good people watching. We ambled north up 3rd Street until we crossed Market Street and she stopped.

"Well, here we are," she said mysteriously.

"Here we are what?" I replied. This was before all the art galleries took over, when Olde City just looked old and grimy.

"Look up," she said.

I looked and saw a tiny swinging sign that read Sneakers. I gasped. I took a few steps back. She laughed. I knew Sneakers was a gay club. I had never been to a gay club. I don't think I had actually ever been to any club.

Let me explain something about Viv. Vivian was one of those girls who seemingly knew everything about everything. Next to her I always felt like a country bumpkin. She spent a lot of time in that fabled and magical place New York City, she "knew" people, and she had famous friends (well, at least one). She had been gay before I even knew what the word meant, and she was glamorous, sophisticated, and experienced.

In high school, we were friends but we were not equals. I trailed in her wake hoping to catch up. It was Viv who figured me out, called me out, and kept my secret for two long years. When we were in school, every gay girl was a closeted gay girl, and she was my one friend who I could talk to about anything.

So Viv, being funny like she was, took me to a gay club, unknowing and unprepared. I was not amused. I was terrified.

"Come on, let's go in," she said casually.

"WHAT!!!" I whispered and hurriedly looked around. I started to walk away hoping nobody I knew would see me.

"Oh stop," she said. "It's not a big deal. Let's just see if we can get in. It's early. I bet the door person is not even on yet."

"Are you crazy? I'm only 17! I'll get carded! Or worse, someone will see me!"

My imagination was running wild. I would walk in and all of a sudden a news crew would burst in and I would be on the news. Or maybe I would run into the aunt I'd always had suspicions about or a neighbor or my English teacher!

My heart was beating frantically. Viv just laughed at me. I kept creeping down the street away from the club. Viv grabbed my hand and tried to pull me towards the door. Across the street two young Latinos were watching. They must have known what kind of club it was because they started yelling, "Don't do it!!" "Don't go in, don't do it!" Viv laughed and yanked on my hand. I planted my feet like a dog and pulled back. Then I fell. Now I was embarrassed. The guys laughed and Viv laughed too.

"Fine! Let's go!" Humiliated and red-faced but with my head held high, I stalked over to the door, grabbed the heavy brass handle and pulled.

Inside it was dark, cool, and almost empty. No door person and no news crew, but I was paranoid and freaking out all the same. We sat at a booth with smooth red leather seats. Viv ordered ginger ales and I tried to collect myself.

Then the worst happened. A woman asked me to dance. A lesbian. A butch lesbian! Short fro, I think a Gumby actually. She was quiet, she was confident. I was flabbergasted. Viv urged me on, the woman was patient, and I went. I stepped into her arms and danced with her. Viv danced with a heavy-set white woman, and our eyes met across the small dance floor. It was all very civil, but it was a big moment for me. I danced with a woman I did not know, and in public! I finally felt like a full-fledged dyke.

Back at the karaoke bar, Pepper is on-stage singing some song I do not know. But she's looking at me, so I smile, bounce my head, and take a gulp of my drink. I try to get back into the mood but I feel bored. I look around. Her friends are having a good time — two are even up dancing. They are a good bunch of friends, I'm just not one of them and I feel a bit lonely. Scanning the bar I don't see anybody I know. The girls coming in are getting younger and younger and head straight back to the stairs so they can get to the dance floor upstairs. They've come to get their grind on.

I order another Jack and Coke and check my phone again — nobody in labor tonight. I sigh, take my drink, and smile as Pepper steps off the stage and straight up into my face. I love it when she's brazen. It gives me the shivers and dissolves that loneliness in one fell swoop.

For the rest of the night, we chill at the bar, chatting, laughing, and flirting. One of her friends gets picked up by the bouncer. We crack up watching their awkward conversation. At midnight, we head on home. Usually I would stay at her place, but she's got to get up early for work and I have a long day tomorrow. We kiss goodbye in the car then I head for home and sleep.

CHAPTER THREE

The next day at work I run into my favorite midwife and mentor, Soledad Garcia. She is the midwife most expectant mothers dream about . . . mid-sixties, a little thick around the waist in a motherly sort of way, strong and confident, but nurturing and knowledgeable. We met when I first started classes at Georgetown. She came in as a guest lecturer to talk about racial and cultural differences in pregnancy and childbirth. Of course I was immediately impressed and in awe of her. She had delivered over 1,000 babies!

When I learned she practiced in Philadelphia, I began to follow her like a groupie, sent e-mails, read her articles in newsletters, and when I was ready, applied for a fellowship at her birth center, Mt. Airy Midwives. That was four years ago. I've been working here ever since. But today she is having a particularly bad day.

"I cannot believe this new hospital policy! Since when do risk managers get to decide how women should have babies! She is a perfectly healthy thirty-year-old, the babies are perfectly healthy, and everything is progressing as it should. And frankly, I know what the hell I'm doing!" Soledad slammed the phone down in her office and stalked down the hall into the OB's offices.

"I'm not blaming you, I just wish there was more support from OBs about this. Women have had twins naturally for years and she's my niece! I don't want her to end up with a C-section."

Dr. Miller quietly closed the door of her office and tended to her irate friend. Drs. Anita and Jeffrey Miller are the OBs in our practice. They actually started the birth center and take on the licensing and administrative duties so the midwives are viewed as the primary caretakers in the practice, and they are the back-up physicians. It helps that they are married and busy with three young children that were all delivered by Soledad.

A few minutes later, Soledad comes out calmer, but with a determined look about her.

"Hey sweetie!" she says and gives me a hug. "Walk with me."

We walk into the kitchenette where she makes a pot of herbal tea and heats up a big bowl of *arroz con pollo*.

"I'm sorry about that, but it just really gets me pissed. How have you been? What about your patient load? Are you able to handle all your clients? Have you checked out the new holistic center we are partnering with? We get free sample massages! I had mine yesterday, but it looks like I'll need another one." She laughs. "How's your love life? You look a little stressed out. Are you getting enough sex or is it too much?" She laughs again.

Soledad does not have time to waste on subtlety. I open my mouth to try and answer at least one of her questions, but she sticks a forkful of her lunch in it and I close my mouth and chew. It's one of my favorite dishes and no one makes it like her.

I start to tune her out when she asks, "Have you seen our newest patient, Candace Wheeler? Isn't she just a hot mess? I've never seen pregnancy sit so awkwardly on a woman before!"

I almost spit out my revered *arroz con pollo*. "Did you say Candace Wheeler? W-W-W-What does she . . . um how many months . . . who sees her . . . wait . . . does she live . . . Candace . . . huh?"

Soledad stops eating and looks at me.

"What in the world is wrong with you, *chica*? You look like you've seen a ghost! Do you know her? I hope I didn't offend you, she's a nice girl, just . . ."

I excuse myself with a wave, and am already out the room and heading to Tracy Ann at the receptionist desk.

"Hi," says Tracy Ann, "your 11 a.m. has just come in; she's in the restroom."

"Uh, OK, thanks," I say. I quickly get myself together and try to sound casual. "Hey, I heard we have a new patient, um, it's the same name of someone I knew, Candace Wheeler?" I squeak. Tracy Ann flips through her appointment book.

"Yes, that's right she's a new client and she's five months along."

At that moment, my patient Anita comes waddling out the bathroom, smiling at me and holding her belly up.

"Only gained another three pounds, Dee. I hope this baby comes right at 38 weeks, I'm tired with this one."

"Hi, Anita. Oh, I expect she'll come at just the right time. Come on in, you look great!"

I hate to say it, but I gave my patient less than my full attention that appointment. Like a drum beat "Candace" pounded in my head. While I examined Anita (Candace), while we talked (Candace), while she asked (Candace), while I answered (Candace), while we chit chatted (Candace) and looked at recent pictures of her other children (Candace) – the last one I delivered (Candace). I hugged Anita good-bye – I'd see her again in two weeks (Candace).

After she left, I sat quietly while the thumping continued and I tried to collect my thoughts. It couldn't be her, haven't seen her, haven't heard from her, nah, it couldn't be. I picked up my phone. My hands were sweaty and a little shaky. I was being ridiculous.

"Tracy Ann?"

"Yes, Dee." This could be a terrible idea. "When is Meadow's next appointment with Candace Wheeler? If it's that same woman, she was a good friend of mine from high school and I'd love to see her again."

"Well," Tracy replies, "her next appointment is in three weeks. But you should talk to Meadow first. She might at least be able to tell you something about her."

Right. Of course, she is off today. I go home but I'm so preoccupied, I don't remember the drive.

Mercifully, Pepper is hanging out with her kid sister that night, so I am alone with a bottle of Sangre de Toro and some jazz. I decide to make some pasta and a simple salad to go with my wine. I put my water on to boil and start chopping carrots. I really haven't thought about Candace in a while, a long while, but I can see her face as clear as day.

We met in Ms. Brown's sophomore English class at Girls' High. I loved English class. I was a big reader and Ms. Brown was on a mission to have us read 25 books in her class. She was a typical looking English teacher. She wore horn-rimmed glasses with a chain, comfortable cable knit sweaters, slacks and loafers. Of all my teachers, I felt that she was the most moved by her own classes. She talked about those books like old lovers. She was affectionate and loving towards them, knew them intimately, and accepted their faults with honesty and tenderness.

I often thought she must be lonely. She wore no wedding ring and had no pictures on her desk, but she always seemed pretty happy. Ms. Brown liked to shake things up. The books she picked covered every kind of genre and while most were classics, she threw in some chick lit, non-fiction, biography, and poetry. No two assignments were alike and occasionally she made us all get up and change our seats.

After the first week in her class, we had to rearrange ourselves into alphabetical order according to first name and introduce ourselves to our new neighbors. The girl in front of me turned around and smiled. I'd seen her before but I'd never talked to her.

"Hi," I said.

"Hey. What's your name again?" she asked.

"Deirdre," I replied, "but everybody calls me Dee".

"OK, I'm Candace and nobody calls me Candy."

I smirked and laughed. She smirked back and turned back around to chat with the girl in front of her. Candace had dark mocha brown skin with surprising freckles and a slightly asymmetrical hairstyle that just reached the top of her shoulders. She wore gold hoops and a gold chain with a charm on it. Her Swatch was big and red and she wore Timberland boots with her tight jeans. When the bell rang, she jumped up, gathered her books, and headed out to the door. She glanced back at me and gave a quick wave. I waved back.

The next day, some girls went back to their old seats. Candace and I did not. We chatted every day until class started. Sometimes we wrote snide comments on our notebooks and showed them to each other. Sometimes we just rolled our eyes at each other when Ms. Brown was being extra theatrical. It was an easy friendship. She was not too put off by my sarcasm and I liked her blunt honesty, even when it was about my clothing choices. I looked forward to English every day.

Occasionally we would hang out in the hallways or at lunch. I liked her a lot, but class schedules, afterschool activities and the school's walls defined our friendship and I was content with that. Sometimes I wondered why she even bothered with me when she already had lots of friends. She was the kind of girl that everybody wanted for a best friend. She was pretty but not too beautiful and smart but not a nerd. She had a twang at times but she was not a troublemaker, and she could be funny without being cruel or obnoxious. I didn't know why she decided to befriend me. I thought maybe it was because I was kind of different.

My high school was one of the best schools in the city. It had a long history of great academics and most of the girls who graduated went on to college. Girls from all over Philadelphia applied to get in so I got to meet girls from outside of my neighborhood, all with different ethnicities, cultures, and economic backgrounds. What we had in common was that we were smart, worked (fairly) hard in school and wanted to go to college, or at least our parents wanted us to. We had a "brother" school down the street. But at least in school, there were less "boy drama" distractions. Of course, just before the bell rang at the end of the day, the bathrooms would be packed to the gills with girls in the mirror putting on make-up and fluffing their hair or patting it down as the case may be.

I wasn't really a loner, but I was alone a lot. I never felt comfortable with a clique and never fell in with one. My closest friends at school were my fellow members of the Health Careers Club, Student Government, and the Spanish Society. *Toda mi vida, yo he adorado el sonido de la música española del idioma y salsa.* I did normal teenage things like sneaking a sip of my Dad's beer, going to roller skating parties, obsessing over music, and worrying about my acne.

I had just broken up with a boy from the neighborhood named John. Our romance only lasted for two months or so. He was cute, but in the end I just didn't care about him too much. We kissed and that was cool. His conversations just got to be boring and he only seemed interested in watching TV. I broke up with him over the phone, gave him back his chain, and never looked back. I had other friends from my neighborhood, but mostly I kept them at a distance. They were into smoking and playing hooky, but I had other plans so I said "hey" and kept on stepping. My mom kept me close to home and I spent a lot of time reading Stephen King books, studying, and listening to music in my room. I felt different, like I had a secret, or a mission or a special destiny. I just didn't know what it was yet.

Winter rolled around and settled in making every day a struggle to get to school and to care once you were there. I've always hated winter. But on a freezing cold Monday morning in January, Ms. Brown looked inexplicably excited. I grumpily wondered what her problem was.

"OK, girls. In honor of our next book, I want you to rearrange yourselves according to the color shirt you are wearing."

There was a lot of grumbling and noise and debate about precise shirt colors but after seven minutes, we were all re-seated and color-coded. I happened to be wearing a red cable knit sweater that day, and Candace was wearing a reddish button down shirt with a faint paisley design. She looked back at me and smiled. She moved over to the seat next to me. At least it would be easier to pass notes now.

I said, "Like your shirt."

"Thanks. Guess we're stuck with each other." She smiled.

"Guess so," I replied, shrugging but feeling pretty happy about that.

Ms. Brown started to pass out our next book. It was *The Color Purple* by Alice Walker. The girls wearing purple looked a little smug.

Ms. Brown announced, "This book has some very mature and difficult subject matter, but I'm really hoping we can tackle it together. It is an amazing, transformative book and I am really looking forward to taking this journey with you."

She was always so dramatic but in this case, she was prophetic. She turned to write our upcoming reading assignments on the board and I flipped open my notebook to copy them down.

When the bell rang, Candace jumped up and met her friends at the door. She smiled back at me. I saluted her, picked up my book, and looked at the cover.

"I think you'll really like this one, Dee," Ms. Brown said.

I looked up at her. "Oh yeah? It looks interesting but I hope it's not about colors."

"No, it's not about colors, it's about one woman's life. It's a hard life but she's a remarkable woman. I hope you'll keep an open mind while reading it."

"OK," I replied wondering what she meant.

The book inspired heated discussion all week long. For educated and "enlightened" girls, Celie's life was just too much for us to take.

The following Sunday morning, I got to page 156 of *The Color Purple* and my life was forever changed. When Shug moves into Celie and Mister's house and Celie begins to fall for Shug, I know something is happening with me. I can feel a buzzing above my ears and a quickening of my heart. I start to re-read it. I read it slowly. I put the book down and walk away. I keep going back and re-reading how their relationship began. I imagine it; I take my time with it. It's like a shawl of knowledge is slowly, gently being wrapped around my shoulders. I understand. I didn't even know it could be.

Tears squeeze out of my tightly closed eyes as it becomes clearer and clearer that this speaks truth to me. I took this terrible journey with Celie and I got to this point and suddenly she, who seemed such a victim and so lost, is smarter than me. I had no idea that loving another girl was even an option. And it just hits me like a ton of bricks. I spend the rest of that Sunday afternoon staring out the living room window and thinking. My mother nags me all morning but I don't hear her. By the afternoon, she gives up and brings me some tea. She glances at the book, says something, and then asks me if she can read it.

Horrified, I yell, "No! Uh it's, uh, it's stupid, it's for school, I haven't finished it, I gotta go." I grab the book and run for my room.

I think and think and think. I think about girls who I really liked but wasn't really friends with, and I think about girls who I was too shy to talk to. I look at the posters on my wall, the ripped out pages of magazines – mostly women, of course Tyson Beckford, but come on! Janet Jackson, MC Lyte, Lisa Bonet, uh oh . . . what if . . . my mind is racing . . . what about that girl at camp this past summer? She tried so hard to be friends with me and I just wouldn't, even though we had so much in common (she wanted to be an obstetrician and loved Stephen King, too!). She made me uncomfortable. She was too pretty. She kept asking me to go to the movies with her.

Was that? Was she? Was I? I couldn't even think the word. It was so clinical, like a disease or something. Did I like girls? Even though I had exhausted myself, I still felt all nervous and jittery inside. I ate a quick dinner and went to bed after I re-read the pages again and again.

The next day I woke up feeling weird and self-conscious. I couldn't stop thinking about me and what if? But I was nervous even thinking about it because I thought maybe people would know what I was thinking. I tried to act normal but acted weird all morning. Awkward, like my clothes were too tight, my shoes were too big and my hair was not done. My voice sounded strained and high to my own ears, so I tried not to talk. I was a mess.

On the bus ride to school, I tried to simultaneously look and not look at the girls and women around me. I walked through the halls of school in a bubble of sound. I spoke to people but was enormously aware of the sound of my own voice. I was sure they could tell what I was thinking about although I was desperately trying not to think about it. And then fifth period came, English class. I reluctantly turned my feet towards class and moved along with the crowd toward Room 305. I could hear my classmates all around me.

"Did you read ...?"

"I can't believe ..."

"That's not right …"

"This book is a trip!"

"I was like, yuck!"

I tried to just move with the flow, keeping my head down and not meeting anybody's eyes. The class was incredibly noisy and boisterous as I made my way to my seat, sat down and took out my notebook. I looked down and got busy doodling. Ms. Brown was just taking her place at the front of the class when Candace rushed in, ducked her head and took her seat beside me.

Ms. Brown waited for her and then said, "Well, I'm so happy to see that most of you have completed your reading assignment for the weekend. I'm looking forward to a very exuberant discussion this afternoon. Before we get started, I want you to look on the board and take note of the final project that is due for this reading. It's a small group project, two or three to a group, and it's due in two weeks. Now, let's get to the book. Reactions?" Hands shot up all around the room.

The next 42 minutes were excruciating. I blushed, got angry, sad, and paranoid. But by the end of it, I was somehow relieved. Some of the girls in my class were even more confused than I was.

"But Ms. Brown, I don't understand. Why is she looking at her like that? Why are they talking about loving each other? They are both women!" cried an exasperated Wendy.

"Ugh, don't be such an idiot! They're dykes!" Tamika hissed venomously.

"Please don't say 'dykes', say 'gay' or 'lesbian'," said Beth. She was head of the Students for Social Awareness and took her job seriously.

"I didn't even know black women could be gay," Sidney said.

My heart skipped a beat when Candace put her hand up. I watched her out of the corner of my eye but she never looked my way.

"I don't know about the whole physical thing, but I know in my life, I'm surrounded by other girls. My mom's a single mom, I have three sisters, am close with my five girl cousins, and my best friends are my heart. I don't know what I would do without my friends who have my back no matter what. Women are strong, we help each other, listen to each other, so I can see how Celie, who never had that, would fall for it," she shrugged.

I nodded and politely smiled. Inside, I felt a little spark ignite inside me.

"Lezzies, bulldaggers, whatever!" said Tamika. "It's disgusting and they should be shot!"

Well, that comment got the rest of the students on the defense. After all, poor Celie had had a hard life. Weren't we in her corner? We debated the issue for almost the whole period. Ms. Brown was well prepared for the wide range of emotions and points of view and managed to keep the conversation somewhat civil. At the end of it, most girls allowed that even if they disagreed with people being gay, Celie deserved some love and happiness no matter where it came from. Some girls however, made it clear that they would never tolerate it. I took mental notes and learned that day about silence.

As the class was leaving, I snuck a look at Candace. She looked thoughtful. Normally we chatted as we packed up. Today, I was quiet. I didn't know what to say.

"Well, that was interesting, huh?" she asked quietly. I nodded and tried not to meet her eyes. My face felt hot. She started to turn and walk away but stopped in front of the board.

"Hey Dee?" she said. I looked up.

"You wanna do this project with me?" she said casually.

"Oh sure," I said equally casual.

"Good." She walked back, took a pen out of her backpack and wrote on the inside of my notebook cover.

"Here's my number, call me so we can talk about it. Bye!" she said waving and walking towards her friends outside the door.

"Bye," I murmured to her back.

I guess it made sense for us to pair up; we were friends in the class. But I was suddenly uncomfortable with the whole idea of it. Was this just a logical extension of our friendship? Did she have suspicions about me and feel sorry for me? Was this some kind of trick? Honestly, I didn't know what to think.

So I decided not to think anything. I was already on information overload. I was in the middle of some kind of emotional upheaval that I couldn't express to myself or anyone else. It was all just too much. That night, I couldn't call Candace. I tried 23 times but I could not think of one thing to say that would not sound fake, phony or forced. I couldn't be myself because I wasn't quite sure who I was anymore. So I just kept reading *The Color Purple* and I finished it.

The next morning I was tired but satisfied. I finally knew how the book ended and it didn't scare me. It gave me hope. I went to school and spent the morning trying to craft my apology. By the time English class rolled around, I was prepared with a white lie of being swamped with homework but it was not necessary. Candace was not mad at me. In fact she seemed pretty bubbly, just chatting away, blowing off my missed phone call and making me give her my number instead since I couldn't be trusted. I was filled with relief. She didn't seem nervous or suspicious at all. I relaxed and almost felt normal again.

That night, she called me. There's something about talking on the phone that lets you open up more than you would in person. That night, all the automatic distance that I put between any potential friend and myself just started to melt away. We talked, really talked. We talked about our families, childhoods, music, and movies. We talked about things we liked, things we hated, and things we really just didn't care about at all. Every night that week, we talked. For me, it was like I'd finally found a friend. A true friend who wanted to know and seemed to genuinely care about what I thought, how I felt, and what I wanted. I was overjoyed.

The following week was the same. As a class, we finished the book and were overjoyed to see Miss Celie exact some revenge and gain some dignity. Candace and I continued our late night phone conversations, though in school we didn't see each other as much. In class on Friday, Ms. Brown reminded us we had the group assignment to complete. From the five choices, Candace and I picked the collage assignment. It seemed the least intimidating and promised the least amount of writing. Plus, Candace said her mom used to be a hairdresser who had kept a ton of magazines we could cut up. We decided to meet Saturday afternoon at her house. She seemed a little nervous. I was excited; I didn't go visiting friends too often. We didn't talk Friday night. She went out to dinner with her family and I watched an old movie with my mom. Friday night was always pizza and movie night at my house.

Saturday morning, I woke up feeling inexplicably anxious. I spilled my orange juice, tripped over my bathrobe, banged my head on the low stairwell, got toothpaste in my nose (which burns!!!!), and tried on seven outfits before I went with jeans, black tank and a purple hoodie (in honor of the book, of course). I called Candace to confirm, got my SEPTA TransPass and headed out with a humongous awkward whiteboard for the collage.

As I waited for the bus, my heart thumping away in my chest, I started to think. *OK, I might like girls. I might like this girl. What am I going to do? I like her as a friend. I like her a lot as a friend. What if we are just good friends, that would be perfect, right? But what if she "knows" something about me? What if I do something stupid and then she decides that she doesn't want to be my friend anymore? What if she's disgusted? What if she doesn't like me that way? (Of course, she doesn't!) What if she gets offended? What if* she beats me up? Or gets her friends to beat me up? What am I thinking? I can never let her know what I think I know about me! She can't like me, right? That's just stupid. A girl like her could never be weird like me.

It was a long bus ride and by the time I got to her house my mind was swirling and my stomach was in knots. I could barely walk. Candace lived in West Oak Lane, close to Washington and Ogontz Avenues. It was a nice looking rowhouse, probably the nicest on the block. Next door, there was a teenage boy with a black hoodie and wool cap sitting on the steps; he gave me the barest of nods. I opened the screen door and closed my eyes as I pressed the doorbell. I could feel sweat drip down my spine.

By the time I opened my eyes, she was flinging open the door and yelling, "Hi! I thought you'd never get here!"

She grabbed my hand and pulled me inside, banging the whiteboard all over the doorway. I smiled, but my stomach was still upset and I tripped into the house. Her mom and sisters were all sitting on the couch with their coats on looking at me. I looked at them, embarrassed and bewildered. They looked restless and curious.

"My mom wanted to meet you," Candace said. "They are all going out shopping but I told them I had a book project to do so I couldn't go." She seemed a bit over-excited.

"Hi," I said offering a polite wave. "I'm Deirdre . . . Armstrong?" I didn't know what to say.

Candace's mom rose and said, "Hi, honey. I'm Ms. Wheeler, this is Denise, Kim and Carrie, Candace's sisters. It's always nice to meet one of Candace's friends. OK then, you two have fun with your assignment, we're off to have fun at Macy's!" She turned to Candace and said, "There's plenty of food in the fridge but leave the chicken alone, that's for dinner tonight, OK?"

"OK, mom. See y'all later. Pick me up something cute," Candace yelled after her sisters who were already half way out the door grumbling about having to wait for something so stupid.

They left and we were alone. I just stood there with my backpack and churning stomach. Candace let out a huge sigh, bit her lip and looked at me.

"Let's put on some music! Are you hungry? Thirsty? There are the magazines," she said pointing to a stack of 30 or so *Ebony*, *Jet*, *National Geographic*, *Black Hair*, *Good Housekeeping*, and *Glamour* magazines. "I thought we could use the kitchen table when we're ready to put it together. Did you bring an extra pair of scissors? I can't remember the last time I used a glue stick. I hope this'll be fun ..." She walked into the kitchen, leaned back and said, "Have a seat. What kind of soda do you like? Orange? Grape? Lemon-Lime?"

"Black Cherry if you have it. Coke is fine if you don't." I sat on the floor near the magazines, took my extra pair of scissors out and started to look through the nearest *Black Hair*. The living room was Philly typical – wall-to-wall rust-colored shag rug, a big beige sectional sofa facing a mirrored wall. There was a small TV in the corner next to a large stereo system. She came back in the room with the drinks and put them down near me on the glass and black lacquered coffee table.

"I looked through some of my mom's music that I thought might get us in the mood for the book and stuff, you know," she stammered. She quickly turned away toward the stereo. I heard a click, and then Billie Holiday's "Lover Man" filled the room. I looked at her. Wait a minute, what was going on here? Maybe *she* liked *me*? She picked up a notebook from the table.

"I thought we should make a list of definite pictures we would like to look for or need for the project." We started to make a list – young girls, babies, words, African landscapes and people, the South, a jukebox, anything purple, a beautiful woman, a bathtub, good food, etc. Then we got to work leafing through the magazines, looking, talking, laughing, and cutting.

When we got to the last couple of magazines, I said, "Too bad we don't have any good pictures of women hugging." Candace shot me a look. "Oh, I mean for her sister, to show her sister and her. They really loved each other, you know." I said.

"Yeah, you're right. We should show something about the love they had for each other. ..." she paused. "But what about Celie and Shug?" she ventured. I shrugged.

"How would we show that?" I asked. "I don't think we're gonna find any pictures of girls kissing in these magazines." I laughed nervously.

"I don't think I've ever seen any pictures of girls kissing ... ever," she said.

"Me either," I said.

She looked in the mirrored wall as if talking to herself, "I wonder what that looks like."

I froze. She looked at me through the mirror. I looked at her. She was waiting for my reaction. I kept my gaze steady. Time froze. I swallowed my panic. It was as dry as the desert and the buzz was back in my ears.

Still staring at the mirror, she slowly reached her hand towards mine. I watched it, but still gasped when I felt her hand. It was warm and smooth. I stroked it with my finger. She turned it over and over slowly; my finger circled her hand. My heart pounded. It was so quiet. Billie had stopped singing.

Still staring into the mirror, she inched toward me, I was fingering up her forearm. She had goose bumps. I could barely breathe. Watching in the mirror, I slowly turned toward her and nudged away the last two magazines between us. She was on her knees, so I got up on mine. We inched closer and closer until my finger had traveled up her arm, onto her shoulder and up her neck, her hand reaching out toward my waist to bring me closer.

Finally, we were inches apart, facing each other with our heads turned to the mirror. I was close enough to smell her. She smelled clean, but warm and spicy like ginger. I was scared but excited. I watched her breathing. I watched her watching us. I watched her expression turn from curious to certain. She licked her lips. My whole body vibrated with anticipation and a sudden want. I leaned forward, watching my lips get closer to hers, I saw her eyes close to half-mast and I kissed her lips gently. I watched in the mirror for a few seconds, then I turned full on to her, closed my eyes and really kissed her. I kissed her softly, slowly, seriously, with my whole being, with unexpected relief, with meaning. She kissed me back, sweetly at first but I could feel her passion growing behind it. Our bodies didn't touch; we kept those inches between us. One step at a time and the kissing was good, good enough to last for hours.

BRRRRRRRrrrrrrrrrrrring! Startled, I almost spill my drink! Laughing at myself, I set down my wine glass and get up to get the phone. That ring is my "patient" ringtone. After 37 weeks, I give my moms my direct number. I know it must be Anita.

"Hello, this is Dee," I say.

"Dee, sorry to bother you but I think I'm having contractions. I had some spicy food today and now my belly is hard and I'm having pain all around the middle. I know I'm supposed to wait for something more regular and consistent but I think this could be it," Anita says hopefully. I am doubtful but agree to meet her at the birth center just in case. I need to get some air anyway.

❧ CHAPTER FOUR ❧

The next morning, I decide to go for a run on Kelly Drive. I'm not a regular runner but I should be. I love running; it makes me feel powerful, capable, and strong. Sometimes I meditate while I run; sometimes I listen to music; sometimes I pray, and sometimes I just appreciate the trees, the flowers, the people and the river running beside me. As I'm pulling on my sweat socks, my phone rings again. It's Pepper. I hesitate, but answer it.

"Good Morn-ting!" I say brightly.

"Hey babe," she says sleepily. "What are you up to today?"

"I'm going for a run. Wanna come?" I ask this knowing she does not like any kind of exercise.

"Nah, I'm just getting up. But would you like to come over when you're done? I'll make us brunch," she says.

"Sure! I'll be there around 11 a.m. OK?"

"Great, see you then." I packed a bag and was off.

My run is perfection. The air is still brisk and clean with the promise of spring to come, the river is sparkly in the morning sun, the sky is a pale blue with those fine wispy clouds I love, and I push myself to three miles. Feeling good, I take a rest on one of the benches and my thoughts turn back to Candace. What if that is her? What if she is

Meadow's patient? What if she's married? What if she's married to a man!?!? What if she's happy? Of course, I want her to be happy, right?

That was so long ago; we were so long ago. I haven't seen her since our senior year in high school 14 years ago. I know she went to Spelman College in Atlanta and I went to Yale University in Connecticut, but we had broken up long before that. The thought of seeing her now makes me … I think I would be too nervous. I know they say you never forget your first love, but we were everything to each other back then. I could not breathe without her, my day didn't begin until I heard her voice and I knew everything was all right in the world. I've had a lot of girlfriends since then, but I never loved anybody the way I loved her. My heart feels heavy as I realize that. I look out on the sparkly water, feel the cool breeze on my face and realize I'm crying. Stupid.

I angrily wipe my tears, shake my head, take a sip of water, and start walking back to my car. That was so long ago and so much has happened since then. I make myself think about Pepper. A fine woman who is making me breakfast right now. A sexy woman, probably still in her t-shirt and panties from last night. A good woman, smart, funny, and possibly with biscuits in the oven. I walk faster, shaking off Candace and the past. By the time I get to my car, I feel better. I turn on the radio, Michael Jackson's "Wanna Be Starting Something" is playing and by the time I get to Pepper's house, I'm hyped to see her.

Pepper opens the door of her University City apartment and smiles at me. Damn, she's already dressed. I smile, step in, close the door behind me and reach for her. We kiss but she pushes me off some.

"Um, breakfast is ready, but you my darling, are sweaty and disgusting. Do you want to take a shower?"

"If you take it with me?" I reach for her again. She sidesteps out of my grip.

"I've had my shower. What has gotten into you?" she laughs.

"What?! I had a good run, I'm feeling energetic and you look so fine and it smells so good in here. Come here," I plead. I grab her hand and bring her close to me. I kiss her passionately. I run my hands slowly up her waist until I cup her breasts. Lightly I finger her nipples and she starts to respond. They get hard under my touch. I walk her backwards towards her couch, slip my hands down onto her sweatpants and slide them down her legs. I kneel before her, just looking at her red bikini panties. Curly black hair poking out around the sides, strong brown thighs under my hands, I slide my fingers up, hook them under her panties and slide them down.

I can hear her sigh. I can smell her musk. I'm wet with anticipation. I poke my nose up in her hair and dip my tongue up. Wet, sweet, peppery. I slowly pull her down so she can sit on the couch, spread her thighs and I go to work. I lick her, slowly, then fast, then slow, I bring her up, take her down, pause and make her thrust her hips up to meet my tongue. She's got her hands in my hair but I don't let her take charge. She swells under my tongue, I know just what to do and when she's just about ready to come, I slip in two fingers and fuck her slowly while I lick her to a growling orgasm. I hold my tongue steady until she stops pulsating under me. Slowly, I withdraw my fingers, my tongue, my face.

She takes my head in her hands, looks me directly in the eyes and says, "I think you need to start running on a regular basis. You hear me? Goodness! You need some new running shoes?" She collapses back on the sofa. I laugh, help her get dressed and head off to the shower.

Pepper and I spend the weekend together, like any couple would. We walk around Rittenhouse Square, and get some Thai food for dinner. We go to the Ritz and watch a weird French film, then go back to her house, and have some good sex. The next morning, we laze around her place, read the paper, check e-mails and Facebook. By late Sunday afternoon, I decide to give my mom a call. She's making pork chops and invites me to dinner. Of course, I accept.

My parents still live in the house I grew up in, so it's always good to go back. I pull up to the red and white twin and marvel at how it hasn't changed at all. I can still see us playing hopscotch and jumping rope in the middle of the street. I can still see the crowd of kids hovering when my next-door neighbor got a busted nose during a fight with Andre from up the block. That was a mess. I wave to the neighbors across the street and head up the walkway. My sister Janine opens the door.

"Hey, sis!" We hug and I go inside. She's three years younger but six inches taller and five shades lighter. We used to make lots of jokes about the mailman when we were younger, but my dad, with his rich brown skin, didn't think it was so funny. Janine has decided to change careers, again. This time, she is going back to school to be a physical therapist. So she's back home, again, living in her old bedroom and complaining about it every chance she gets. I can smell the candied yams, macaroni and cheese and asparagus before I even turn the corner into the kitchen. There's Mom at the sink, washing something in the apron I gave her 10 years ago for Christmas. I give her a hug and see what I can do to help.

After dinner, my dad goes back to the TV room to watch a basketball game and my mom, sister, and I chat in the kitchen. Janine talks about school, I talk about work, and my mom talks about the neighborhood and her impending retirement. It's all warm and cozy and familiar until Janine lets out a gasp.

"What?!" my mother and I ask, my mother alarmed, and I annoyed.

Janine sighs and says, "Dee, I forgot to tell you. I saw one of Candace's sisters the other day. I think it was Denise."

"Janine, is that all? Why do you have to be so dramatic? You're going to give me a heart attack!" my mother exclaims.

"Oh, how is Denise?" I say trying to sound casual, trying to still the sudden drumming of my heart.

"She's fine. Just got divorced, I think. She had two kids with her who were acting up so we didn't get to talk long," says Janine.

"Oh…. How's their mom? Her other sisters? Candace?" I say as casually as I can manage. My mom sneaks a glance at me. I see it.

"Like I said, we didn't get to talk much, but she's working at the library. I think she's a librarian at the Coleman Library," Janine replies. But she's looking at me funny.

"I'm just asking. I was just curious. Can't I just be curious? Sheesh!" I say all annoyed. Inside my heart is just drumming away (Candace). "I'm gonna go watch the game with Dad." They watch me leave, shrug and continue cleaning up.

I go sit with my dad, pour myself a small snifter of cognac and tune in to the game. The Sixers and Nets. My dad and I exchange small talk about the game, the cognac warms me up and I relax. I think back to when I came out to him in this very room.

I was 21 and a senior on winter break . . . my last winter break. We were watching football. Well, he was watching it. I had a book in my hand but mostly I was thinking about how I would say what I had to say. My dad is the quiet type. He has opinions, lots of them, but he keeps them mostly to himself. I had no idea what he thought about gay people. I had no idea if he even knew what that was. It just wasn't anything that ever came up in conversation and he didn't know any gay people as far as I knew. I wasn't scared. I didn't think he would disown me, or yell at me, or make a big fuss. That was not his style. I just didn't want him to think less of me, to be disappointed or disgusted by me. And I had no idea of how to start this conversation.

"Dad," I said.

"Mmmm? Oh! Oh! Fumble! Unbelievable!"

"Dad," I said again trying to muster up the courage to just dive in and say it. "Would you be upset if I didn't get married? Or have kids?"

"What? What are you talking about, Deirdre?" he asked turning his head slightly towards me but keeping his eyes on the screen.

"I might not ever get married or have kids. Is that OK with you?" I was starting to get emotional.

"Deirdre, you have to live your own life. If you don't get married or have kids, that's up to you. I don't have a say in that. Why are you worried about that? You should be thinking about graduation and what you're going to do after that. That's what's important now, right?" He looked at me.

"I'm gay," I said looking back at him. He sat quietly looking at me. I started to tear up waiting for him to say something.

"Are you sure about this?" he asked.

I shook my head. "I'm sure daddy, I'm sure…. Do you hate me?" I asked.

"I could never hate you, Deirdre, you're my daughter. If you're sure about this, then OK. Like I said, you have your own life to live and you have your own choices to make. If this is what you want, then OK. I love you no matter what. OK?"

"OK," I replied and wept from relief. I never loved him more. He got up and hugged me but I could see his eyes sliding towards the screen. It made me love him even more. I closed my eyes and hugged him hard.

Ten years later, I look over at my dad. He's aged a bit, more gray hair, more sagging jaw, more wrinkles on his hands, but he's the same – steady, consistent, and reliable. I tear up again thinking about how lucky I am. Suddenly, he lets out a huge snort. I bust out laughing when I realize he's over there napping.

❧ CHAPTER FIVE ❧

Monday morning and I'm back at work. I see Meadow as soon as I walk in the door.

"Good morning, Meadow!"

"*Namaste!*" she replies and bows to me.

"*Alaikum salaam,*" I bow back. We laugh. She's one of my favorite people. She's as crunchy as they come but she doesn't take herself too seriously. Today she's wearing some kind of maroon and beige dashiki and a headband with a white feather. It could be very corny but she actually makes it looks kind of stylish. We head back to the offices together.

"So you were inquiring about one of my patients?" she asks over her shoulder.

"Yeah, the name sounds very familiar to me and I just wanted to make sure she wasn't a girl I was friends with in high school," I reply.

"Well, you're in luck. She just happens to be stopping by today to pick up some handouts and a 'script' for iron."

Thump. Thump. "Oh, cool. Let me know when she gets here." My stomach instantly knots up. I go into my office, close the door gently behind me and stare at one of my favorite paintings, Georgia O'Keefe's "Pelvis IV" to try to calm myself down. Breathe. Whew. OK. Then I look in the mirror because if I'm going to see my first love, I've got to look good. I pat the hair, re-curl some curls, take out a gloss and glide it over my lips. My hands are shaking a little.

I put on some Norah Jones and prepare for my patient, Missy and her husband George. They should be 35 weeks today. This should be fun. George is an ex-boyfriend of my sister's. He's a good guy and comes to every visit. I think he's a little nervous with me being a lesbian and having my hands all up his wife. I don't know how to explain it, but looking at my patients' body parts is nothing at all like looking at a lover's. When I am at work, I am all business and patient care. I love pregnancy and I love pregnant women, but bodies can be very clinical for me and at heart, I'm a scientist. Most of the time, I have to remember to switch it off when I'm not working. Nobody wants a Pap smear when they're making love.

After my third patient of the day, I hear a knock at the door.

"Hey, it's Meadow. Candace is here." I had almost forgotten! My stomach knots return and I get up and open the door. Meadow points down the hall to reception. I see a figure in a green down coat bending over and picking up something. I start down the hall, and she stands back up and turns toward me. She smiles and says, "Hello!"

I am looking over her shoulder, scanning the waiting room but no one else is there. She continues to stare at me. "Hi! I'm Candace. You wanted to meet me?"

Like a popped balloon, I deflate. It's not her. It's not my Candace. It's not even close. This is a very thin white woman with an impossible large belly. I try to recover my manners and stretch out my hand.

"Hi. I'm Dee Armstrong. I did want to meet you. You have the same name as a girl I was close with in high school. I was hoping to see her again." I try to laugh it off, but I know I sound disappointed.

"Oh. Well I'm pretty sure we didn't go to high school together. I would have remembered you! Sorry I'm not your friend, but nice meeting you anyway," she says. And with that, the fake Candace Wheeler picked up her papers and wobbled out.

⁂

For two weeks, I pouted. I did my thing at work, but at home I grew increasingly dejected. Pepper had no idea what was wrong with me. She tried many wonderful and creative things to bring me out of my mood. And while they worked temporarily, after the moment was over, I lapsed back into my funk. I grew increasingly annoyed with her, with her name, with her friends. I tried another run on Kelly Drive but I couldn't even make a mile. I wandered, I stumbled, the river looked gray and dirty, and the air was chilled.

Then on a Saturday night, having declined Pepper's invitation to go out and dance, I was home having some baked chicken and potatoes watching *Terms of Endearment* for the fifth time. You can't go wrong with Debra Winger and Shirley MacLaine! Straight drama!

BRRRRRrrrrrrriing! I pick up the phone. It's Anita.

"Dee, Dee! This is it! She's coming. I felt pains. I waited. I wanted to be sure. But now ARRUURRGGH!!!!!!!!"

I wait until the contraction passes. "Anita, how far apart are the contractions?"

"Eight, no that was six, six minutes apart. I'm so nervous! Oh, my gosh. I passed my mucous plug this morning so I knew it was coming, I'm so excited!!!!"

"Great, OK. I'll meet you at the birth center. Don't forget your birth plan and all the things you wanted for relaxation. And your camera, Anita, remember last time?!"

"Check, check, check!!! Thanks, see you there!" I grab my purse, my food/snack bag, and a change of clothes. My adrenaline was pumping. It was time for Anita to finally have her baby!

Sunday night, I was holding a sleepy seven pound, eight ounce perfect little girl, Maria Dorothy James. Anita was napping and her boyfriend Rashid was out getting food and texting friends and family. I was holding this new little life, whom I had known since she was a tiny growing embryo, barely 10 weeks conceived. I watch her little nostrils breathe in and breathe out. I watch her little mouth pucker. I watch her open one eye and peek at me. And all my depression washes away under the enormity of the miracle of her birth. I'm an idiot sometimes. I had been so focused on my disappointment with what didn't happen that I didn't see the obvious. I needed a change.

Feeling renewed and refreshed on Tuesday morning, I call and ask Pepper over for dinner. She agrees but seems a little hesitant. She asks me if I'm out of my funk and I tell her I am. I apologize for being such an ass and promise to thank her with a home-cooked meal.

There is something else I need to do too, and it is not going to be easy. I don't say it to myself, I don't even think it to myself. But when the universe makes things plain to you, you'd best not wait to make the changes you need to make.

Tuesday evening arrives and I cooked my favorite dinner, Jamaican curry chicken, fried plantain, and some coco bread I picked up earlier in the day. I had ginger beer and rum ready for drinks, and some pineapple upside down cake with coconut ice cream for dessert. I put on Bob Marley, light some candles and incense, and relax. Pepper knocked on the door, late as usual, and laughs when I open it.

"You went all out, huh? You must be feeling pretty guilty for the crappy way you've been treating me," she smirks.

She's a little more dressed up than usual, like she is trying to impress me or maybe shame me for my stupid behavior. Either way, the low cut red blouse, the tight black maxi skirt with the thigh-high split and the black leather boots are exceedingly distracting. I look down at my usual jeans and Henley and feel a bit underdressed. At least I have on my Jamaican knit cap for some flair. I need a drink.

"Come on, mon, let's eat," I say in my best Jamaican accent. I hold out my hand, and she takes it and follows me into my tiny dining room. We eat by candlelight, talking and laughing the whole way through. She forgives my moodiness and I finally feel at ease. I take a deep breath.

"Pepper," I say. "I have something I need to tell you." She stops eating, her fork midway to her mouth with a piece of cake on it. She looks at me.

"What, babe? What's wrong?" she asks.

She looks so genuinely concerned I almost forget what I'm saying. She's looking at me as if she loves me. Does she love me? I hadn't even thought of that before. Oh my God, I haven't really thought about her feelings much at all, have I? I'm such a selfish, self-absorbed ass. I am and I know it. It almost makes this easier.

"You deserve better than me," I say quietly. The cake drops off her fork as she lowers it to the plate. The piece of cake rolls on the table and stops between us. I resist the urge to clean it up.

"I like you a lot, I think you are a great person, but I'm not in love with you. You deserve better than me, more than me," I say.

I feel the air change in the room, like the pressure has dropped. I see her face go through a series of emotions. She says nothing. She's staring at me, her lips pressed together, holding back.

"You're breaking up with me?" she says incredulously. "Unfuckingbelieveable! You are really breaking up with me?! Right now? What was this? My last meal? Are you kidding me?" The sarcasm is starting to creep up into her voice. I brace myself for the storm but there is silence instead.

"Are you seeing someone else?" she says suspiciously. Her eyes start darting around the room looking for evidence.

"No," I say. "I'm not seeing anybody else."

"Then what is this? I don't get it. What's the problem? We get along fine, don't we?" She sounded genuinely confused.

"We do and you're great but I … I just want more. I think we have a good relationship, but I want more. I want to be in love," I say pathetically. I sound like a ridiculous teenager even to my own ears.

"Now you don't love me? You know what? This is bullshit. Fine. If you don't want me, I'll go but I think you're either lying or stupid. We have a good thing; most people would kill for a relationship like ours. But if it's not good to you, then I guess it's not good at all. Oh, this is so stupid," she says.

"I know. I'm sorry. I just, I just think there's more out there and I think that we've settled with each other and we got comfortable," I reply trying desperately to make her understand. Pepper stands up, irritated.

"Hey, speak for your own fucking self. I didn't settle. I love you and I love being with you and I thought we could be good for a long time. If you are not happy, that's on you, but don't put any of that shit on me. This is your decision, not mine," she says. She walks to the door, picks up her purse, opens the door, and gives me one last long look.

"I'm sorry," I say, standing up and walking towards her.

"I think you are making a huge mistake, Dee. I really do. Bye," she says and slams the door behind her.

I stand there for a while debating whether I should change my mind and run after her and tell her that it was all a big mistake. But as the seconds ticked by, my doubt dissolves and I know I did the right thing. I know there is something more for me out there. I try but I can't stop myself. I think about Candace.

After our first kiss, which lasted about an hour I think, Candace and I just looked at each other. What we had just done was inconceivable, unbelievable, unprecedented (in our world) and incredible. It was like we had crossed into an unknown universe. Could we breathe there? What language should we use to speak? Who lived here and how?

We had a moment of opportunity where we could take it all back. Get angry with each other for doing something we didn't want to do. We could even get into a fistfight about it and that would put a stop to everything. Or we could laugh it off like a crazy and wild practical joke. We could blame Ms. Brown and Alice Walker for putting these ideas into our heads.

I think all these things went through my mind. But I couldn't do it. I could not deny the hour of perfect affection and passion I'd just spent. I could not deny how wonderfully right it had felt. I could not deny that I *liked* Candace and thought she was beautiful. I could not deny that I wanted that kiss. I had not planned it nor even anticipated it. She offered the possibility of it and I could not deny it. I didn't regret it either, at least not yet. So we looked at each other thinking our thoughts, deciding if we should fight or flee. But we did neither. We stayed.

I said, "Hi."

She giggled. "Hi."

It was exactly as if we were meeting each other for the first time. We saw each other out of our new eyes, and we saw each other newly. We were the same girls but changed.

"I've never done anything like that before," I said shyly.

"Me neither," she replied, "but there's something about you, Dee."

"Me?"

"Yes, you. I really like you," she said, shrugged and blushed. Unbelievable. "Now, if you don't mind, I have got to go to the bathroom and we'd better finish this project before my mother gets home. We'll need that table for dinner." So we got up and got back to work with this new thing between us.

I went home that day on the fabled Cloud Nine. I don't recall much of the journey, only that I couldn't stop smiling and going through the whole day over and over in my mind. I would get to that kissing part and just cheese all over the place. I'm sure the other people on the bus thought I was crazy. I floated off the bus, up the street, down my block, into my house, and up to my room where I immediately called Candace and we spent the rest of the night on the phone. It was great.

Reality set in on Monday morning. I'd felt like a freak for days wondering if people could tell I was having "unnatural" thoughts about girls. Well, now I had actually committed "unnatural acts" with a girl, and you couldn't tell me it wasn't written all over my face. I'd kissed a girl. I liked a girl. I thought she was all that and a bag of chips. I could not tell a soul.

Gratefully, I didn't see Candace until our English class. We got to class, we acted normal, we didn't touch, and we didn't make a lot of eye contact. We passed a note or two, but we were cool, cool, cool. I would look at her and think about what we did and I would blush to myself.

We handed in our project with a hint of regret. Our collage project got an A and a week later our class moved onto another book. But I carried *The Color Purple* in my book bag for weeks afterward. I liked having those characters near me for comfort as we tried to figure out what we were doing.

In my school at that time, no one was gay. There were rumors about this or that teacher and there was teasing about certain girls who were deep into sports. But no one,

NO ONE, was openly gay. It was not accepted, it was not OK, and it could get you hurt.

We knew that and I know we would never have claimed to be gay anyway. We liked each other and that's as much as we would admit. One time, someone had anonymously put a few fliers up in the hallways for a gay teen support group. There was an immediate and vicious negative reaction to it. Girls threatened to beat up whoever did it; they ripped the flyers down and tore them into shreds. That happened when I was a freshman, but I never forgot it. And while I never connected myself with the flyers, I always felt sorry for that poor soul who was brave enough to try and offer help to someone else. She overestimated her classmates' compassion; she underestimated their fear and intolerance.

At school, outwardly we maintained our friendship, we chatted in English class, and sometimes we met to say "hi" or pass notes between classes. But Candace had her group of friends and they had their routines. She came to school with her best friend Shari in the morning and took the bus home with her after school. There wasn't a lot of room for me to fit in there, and the few times she tried to include me, even in a conversation, her friends just looked at me dismissively. She was their friend and they were not too accepting of new girls. I was busy with all my after school clubs and responsibilities, and I had a few friends too who expected my sarcastic comments at lunch.

Thus, we began our covert romance. I will admit that the secrecy of it, the sneaking around, the danger of discovery was thrilling to me. We devised a code so we could pass love notes undetected. We stealthily shared mix tapes, poems, and pictures expressing our feelings for each other. Some days we arranged to wear purple on the same day. It was our secret declaration of love.

Not often, but maybe once a week, we would sneak into an empty classroom and kiss. Sometimes, we kissed in the bathrooms, once in the gym. It was illicit, it was dangerous, and it was exciting. We conducted much of our affair on the phone, at night. We revealed our deepest thoughts and fears, we did our homework together, we watched television together, we listened to music together, and sometimes we just breathed together and occasionally fell asleep together. Our nights were intimate, our days were spent in cloak and dagger machinations. But I'd never felt so alive.

And me and Candace, in the bubble of our little relationship, were blissful. The more I looked at her, the more beautiful she became in my eyes. I counted and cherished her freckles, her one crooked tooth, her long neck, her deep brown eyes, and her surprisingly strong hands.

The more we talked, the more I fell for her. She was compassionate and caring, she was smarter than I'd realized, and she was a lot quirkier than she let on. She had an image of this regular, 'round the way girl that she maintained with a vigilance. But in private she could be unconventional. I found out that she secretly loved rock music and ska, Fishbone, Living Color, and Bad Brains. She also loved horror movies, post-modern art like Keith Haring and Jean-Michel Basquiat (I had never heard of them) and she had a weird interest in the occult.

She was a "good" girl for her mother, and made sure that she fit in with all her sisters and cousins. She didn't disappoint, she did her chores, kept up her grades and didn't cause anybody any trouble. She had easily steered clear of boys because her mother was a church-going woman and she wasn't allowed to date or have a boyfriend. Candace was experienced when it came to having a secret life.

On the weekends, we were able to be together, a little. We spent a lot of time wandering Fairmount Park, looking for privacy, making out when it was safe. Sometimes we went to the movies, sometimes we wandered around downtown, walking slowly past gay bookstores, not having the nerve to enter but giggling at the titles nevertheless. We ate at Chick-fil-a and spent a lot of time at the Gallery, going from store to store.

In public, Candace became my best friend; in private she was my girlfriend. My heart would swell at the mere thought of her; everything I saw, heard or experienced related in some way to her, reminded me of her. My desire to be with her was insatiable. It was sweet, it was all encompassing, and it was almost painful in it's keenness. I had never been so happy, so loved, so understood, and so complete. I was resplendently in love.

❧ CHAPTER SIX ❧

A week later, I feel a little sluggish from the red wine I had last night. But I eat a good breakfast, drink some fresh OJ, and do a 10-minute cardio with five minutes of meditation and I'm good to go. I get to the office and see Soledad helping a couple into their car with their newborn. An "It's a Boy" flag hangs from the window upstairs. I give a wave to the new parents and watch them drive away at five miles per hour. I turn to Soledad. She looks tired.

"Long night?" I ask.

"It was. She labored 12 hours at home and another eight here, but she hung in like a trooper. I'm tired but not as tired as her." Soledad jerks her thumb towards the car finally rounding the corner.

"I'll make some fresh coffee for you," I say sympathetically.

"Nah, thanks, *hija*, but I'm going to take a nap. I don't have a patient until noon," Soledad says quietly. I look at her from the corner of my eye. She seems older in this pale morning sun. Her skin looks looser, her voice trembles a tiny bit, and she walks with some effort. I open the door for her and we go in.

My first patients arrive 20 minutes later. On time and bubbly as usual, Laurie and Leslie bounce through my office door grinning and laughing. I don't know why their apparent happiness gets on my nerves, but it does. I make an effort to be super-pleasant.

"Good morning! Four months already! Let's see how we're doing."

I examine Laurie and all is going well with the pregnancy. I ask them if they have any questions.

"Well," chuckles Leslie with that deep infectious laugh, "we do have an off-topic question for you."

"Oh?" I say. "What's up?"

"Yeah, we have a friend…. Well, sorry, I hope this isn't too nosey, but are you single by any chance?" asks Laurie.

I hesitate. "Well, actually I do happen to be single right now, but I'm not really looking for anything…."

"Oh great!" gushes Laurie. "One of our best friends is single, and we mentioned you and she seemed really interested. Of course, we don't know you, *know you*, but she's a really great person, an artist, very cool, and we thought that, you know…."

"But only if you're interested," interjects Leslie.

"Yeah, I don't know," I demure. "I just got out of something and I don't think I'm looking to meet anybody right now."

"Oh, OK." Laurie sounds dejected. "Sorry to get so personal but we love fixing up our friends. I think we just want everybody to be as happy as we are. We feel so blessed right now."

Laurie stares into Leslie's eyes and kisses her. Leslie rubs her belly and, still smiling, kisses her back. I fight the urge to vomit while keeping my smile in place. Like a goddamn Hallmark card these two! They hug and kiss me good-bye. I am uncomfortably aware of Leslie's shoulder muscles as I wrap my arms around her. She must work out a lot! Whew! They leave and I turn on some Badu to write up my notes.

Why do they bother me so? I should totally love them and be happy for them and I am. But I think I resent them, too. How can they possibly be so happy? Maybe it's a front for the public or maybe they're secretly miserable. But somehow, I don't think so. I think they are genuinely in love. Their life is happening, they are living the dream, married to their partner, having a baby, creating a family.

And I am a part of their plan. I will provide them with the knowledge and confidence they need to have the birth experience they want and will remember the rest of their lives. I am instrumental to helping them achieve their family, their way. It is a big responsibility and I am more than up to the task. I am smart, powerful, and resourceful and I know what my patients need. They need me, and I want to do this for them.

Then why do they get on my nerves so much???

I see the way Laurie looks at Leslie, the trust and love in her gaze and it suddenly reminds me of the way Candace used to look at me. She had that same smile, that relaxed confidence, her face glowing with that same quiet joy … That's it! I know what I need to do. I need to find Candace.

It's so stupid, I know. It's so cliché, I know. But suddenly, I can't get it out of my head. I need to know what happened to her. Where is she? What is she doing? Is she with somebody? Does she regret what happened? Does she ever think of me? Did she really stop loving me?

As soon as I get home that night, I call my sister and ask her to meet me for a drink. She immediately agrees and we decide to meet at Crimson Moon on Sansom Street. Crimson Moon is one of my favorite coffeehouses. Brightly painted and covered with artwork, it's heavily populated with hip-hop artists, students, actors from the theater across the street, and dancers from the studio next door. They're always playing some kind of acid house and serve the best lattes and root beer floats.

Janine arrives soon after I get a table looking out onto the busy street below. Sometimes it's hard to remember that this tall fashionista is my little pipsqueak sister. When did she grow up to be a woman? We hug hello and order from our cute, but way too young for me, waitress. With our chai teas and apple turnovers, we chitchat and catch up with each other. I finally tell her my plan to find Candace. She blows up.

"WHAT!!! Are you out of your mind? After all that drama back in high school? Why in the world would you want to see her?" cries Janine.

"I want to know what happened to her. I used to be so in love with her and now, I have no idea where she is or what's she's doing. It's been almost 15 years and I ... I just want to talk to her," I reply.

"Dee, seriously, I think it's a bad idea. You have so much going for you now, your career, your apartment, you have Pepper...."

"I don't have Pepper. We broke up," I say.

"Well, you'll have somebody else soon enough. You always do," she shrugs.

"Hey, what does that mean?" I ask, indignant.

"It means, big sis, that you never have a shortage of girlfriends coming and going. Which is what I'm saying, why bother going back there? You've been with a ton of women since then, and I'm sure there are plenty more to come," she says.

"Yeah, maybe that's a problem.... She was my first love, Janine."

"Yes, I remember vividly, but come on ... everyone is nostalgic about their first love. I would still drop my panties for Mike in a heartbeat. It doesn't mean we should try to relive those times. You've changed a lot since then, and she probably has too."

"Maybe, I just can't stop thinking about it though," I say. "I just need to know whatever happened to her.... You

said her sister works at the Coleman Library, right?" Janine
nods and sighs, exasperated.

It takes me more than a week to get over to the library.
I got busy at work and then I had to perform the
ceremonial "return of the stuff" ritual with Pepper. It was a
little harder than I had anticipated. She was emotional and I
started to doubt myself again, but it was done and we were
over.

I also had to work up the nerve to see Denise again.
The last time she and I spoke, she hated me. But I assumed
that after all these years we'd be able to have a civil
conversation. I was wrong about that. Dead wrong.

I'm quite familiar with the Coleman Library. It's on the
busy corner of Greene Street and Chelten Avenue. I used
to change buses there everyday to get to and from school. I
also kissed Candace in the bathroom and in the stacks
there. I have a brief flashback of that as I walk through the
doors. It's been renovated since I've last visited. It looks
bright and clean and new.

I walk in and look behind the main desk. I don't see
anybody resembling Denise. I walk over towards the offices
looking casually…. No Denise. I decide to head downstairs;
maybe she works in the Children's section. I venture down
the spiral staircase, but no Denise. I resist going into the
stacks to browse and head back upstairs. I guess I'll have to
ask somebody. I head to the main desk, and a woman
pushing a cart through the aisles almost bumps into me. I
look up. She is wearing a bright red sweater and tweed
pants with her hair pulled back into a bun, but I would
know that face anywhere. It's Denise.

"Hi," I say.

"Hello," she says brightly. Then I see recognition
dawning on her. She makes a small hissing noise and steps
back.

I continue on. "Denise! It's so good to see you. I guess you remember me? Dee Armstrong," I say. I pause.

She says, "Of course I remember you. Dee."

Inwardly, I sigh. I guess bygones will not be bygones today. I reach into my purse for my business card. "I was hoping to get in touch with your sister, with Candace. I haven't seen her in years and...."

"Let me stop you right there," she says, her voice full of old anger. "*No*, I will not get you in touch with Candace, *no*, I do not want your business card, and *no*, I will not pass the information on to her. *We* do not want anything to do with you again. Ever!"

And with that she wheeled the cart past me and never looked back. A couple of patrons cast furtive glances my way. Embarrassed and chagrined, I skulk out of there without another word. Denise had always been the nicest of the sisters, the peacemaker. If she still hates me, then I'm guessing I will not have much luck with any of Candace's family. I head home to come up with a new plan.

Thankfully at home, I have a voice message from one of my best friends, Bernadette "Downtown" Brown. She wants to meet for dinner and tell me something important. Great! I could use a distraction.

Bernadette and I have been friends since college. She was also a Biology major so we had a lot of the same classes. And when we graduated, she decided go to medical school at Temple University here in Philly. We were roommates for four years. I doubt there's anybody who knows me better than her. But with her practice and my practice, we don't get to see each other in person much anymore. This must be big news.

I hardly get through the door of The Continental when I'm nearly blinded. There was a huge glare off the big rock on her finger. As I made my way to the table, I look, I point, I cover my mouth, and gasp dramatically. She squeals, hugs me, and tells me to stop being ridiculous and making a big deal about it. But I know her. She WANTS a big deal made of it.

"OOOhhh girl! That is the most beautiful ring I have ever seen," I gush. I hold her hand up and inspect. It is a mighty big but mighty beautiful stone, maybe two carats. She blushes and preens.

"OK, tell me the whole proposal story, all of it!" I say.

Over Cosmopolitans, pad thai, shoestring fries, and dumplings she lays out the week-long proposal her boyfriend of seven years concocted. It's a little over the top for me with the hot air balloon, praise dancers and flash mob and all. But Darryl knows her and she was successfully blown away. I'm genuinely happy for her and she is just glowing. I guess it could be the spa getaway but she looks fantastic. Dark brown skin gleaming, locks oiled and tight, jewelry sparkling, clothes fitting just right, and I think I detect a hint of perfume.

I am starting to feel kind of frumpy. My hair is looking more frizzy than curly, I have a period pimple on my chin, and I'm probably carrying the back to nature midwife thing a little too far with this poncho and frayed jeans. I wish I had at least cleaned my earrings; they are looking a little tarnished lately. She interrupts my self-conscious reverie by taking my hand.

"Dee Armstrong?" she says seriously.

"Yeeessss?" I say suspiciously.

"Would you do me the honor of being one of my bridesmaids?" She looks at me expectantly.

I smile. "Bernadette Bernie Downtown B-Money Brown, of course. I would be delighted to be your bridesmaid," I say with a slight bow.

"Good! Now my sister is the maid of honor, but we both know how she is." She reaches into her purse and pulls out a notebook with stuffed with papers. Here's what I have so far, tell me what you think."

We spend the rest of the evening so engrossed in her wedding plans I forget to tell her that I'm looking for Candace.

❨ CHAPTER SEVEN ❩

Saturday morning, spring has sprung, and my townhouse is filled with early morning light. My townhouse makes me feel like a grown-up. I bought it just as this neighborhood was being gentrified. It's completely renovated from an old brownstone – hardwood floors, moldings, built-in bookshelves, even a stained glass window in my bathroom with a skylight! But it's got all the good modern conveniences as well, microwave, laundry nook, and kitchen island sink.

I decorated my house in all the colors I love – plums, sage greens, and sky blues. It's colorful but soothing. My bedroom, I painted an interesting mauve. With certain lights on, it becomes an intense red, with other lights on, it's a warm and cozy eggplant. I like to have options. This morning I woke up in my cozy queen bed alone. It was quiet, peaceful, and comfortable. I got up and made myself breakfast, read the paper, played some samba, called my mother, and looked out onto the magnolia tree in bloom. Then I smacked myself on the forehead. Ugh!

I'm dumbfounded at how the obvious has eluded me. I get my laptop. I google Candace and get nothing, just a mention on a list as a Spelman – so I know she graduated but that's about it. But then…. Vaguely I remember hearing from a friend of a friend of a girl who someone used to date that one of Candace's friends from high school owns a hair salon. I decide to give it a try. I google Shari Charles and the shop, Hair We R, comes up with mixed reviews, a coupon, and an address in West Oak Lane. Sweet! I need my hair did anyway. Am I crazy enough to try and go on a Saturday? Yes! Did they have any appointments? No! I make it for next Thursday.

Feeling quite pleased with my detective work, I check my e-mail next and there's one from Laurie and Leslie inviting me to a "ladies party" at a restaurant in the Loews Hotel tonight. They casually mention that their artist friend will be there. I usually try to keep my personal and professional life separate, so I'm a little hesitant. But what the hell, I have nothing planned tonight. Besides, I'm feeling a little adventurous. I take off for a run feeling optimistic, hopeful even.

⚜

That night, remembering my frumpy dinner with Bernie, I try to dress up a little. I find a low-cut white blouse, a push-up bra, and the black dress pants that make my ass look spectacular. And I add a touch of eyeliner and gloss. I don't want to try too hard, but I want to be noticed. In the back of my mind, I'm imagining greeting Leslie, maybe having a casual drunken dance with her, and accidentally falling into her arms. But what I'm telling myself is that this could be a great networking opportunity – lesbians are having babies now – and anyway, this artist chick might be cool. You never know.

I arrive at the party and instantly feel like I've made a mistake. This is not my usual artsy crunchy, activist, home girl lesbian crowd. This is a high-income, executive, affluent, and influential lesbian crowd. On one side of the room is city's Director of Human Relations and her wife, on the other side is a local TV anchor, in the corner is the owner of Marlene's, and the CEO of a Philadelphia-based food distribution service is ordering from the bar. These are serious women who have made it on their own terms. They have power and influence and money. I am feeling short and self-conscious, even with my heels on and hair blown out. I head over to the bar to get my bearings and a Jack and Coke. *Oh, maybe I should drink wine? Champagne?* I think to myself and laugh. Great! Now I look crazy.

"Jack and Coke, please," I order when the bartender finally notices me. Even she looks way out of my league. Get yourself together, Dee! I boost my confidence by thinking about the most academic and cerebral paper I wrote in college (I'm smart!), then
I think about that last very healthy, very beautiful baby I delivered (I'm magical), and then I think about the last time I had sex with Pepper. I knocked her socks off! (I'm hot!). Smiling, I take a sip of my drink and survey the room.

I see Leslie and Laurie making their way over to me with a very gorgeous woman trailing slightly behind them.

"Hi, I'm so glad you could make it!" says Laurie, her dimples just dimpling, her hug taking the breath out of me. Though her baby bump is just barely visible, she is truly radiant with this pregnancy.

"Hey, so good to see you out of the office!" adds Leslie. I am painfully aware of her muscular body through her thin silk blouse as we hug hello. As they fall into line, arms around each other, making a lovely picture, Leslie turns and gestures the other woman forward.

"This is Noema," says Laurie. "Noema, this is Dee Armstrong, our midwife and protector of all things we hold dear and sacred." I give Laurie the side eye and smile, extending my hand to Noema.

"Pleased to meet you," I say.

She shakes my hand and says, "Nice to meet you too. I've heard a lot about you." She is an interesting mix of funky artist and high society chic. She is slightly taller than me, and a couple shades lighter. She has a nose ring and I can see a tattoo climbing up the back of her neck. She's got that corkscrew sandy brown hair, but it's tamed and piled up in a neat bun on her head. Her jewelry, though chunky and colorful, looks expensive. Her dress, while giving off a Mexican peasant vibe ripe with colors and stripes, definitely looks well made and luxurious. She's also checking me out, so I try to look confident but gracious yet still fun. I wonder about how big that tattoo is and how low does it go?

They order cocktails and we all make small talk. I find out that Noema is a painter, a sculptor, and a gallery owner. I also find out that she is immensely popular as we are interrupted a dozen times by various women all seeming to have a compelling interest in her artwork. I exchange business cards with her and she, Leslie, and Laurie move on to mingle.

I end up talking with a few women, handing out my business cards to those who seem interested in my services. Those women who were not immediately interested in childbearing, however, seem to have little to say to me at all. It's as if I am more part of the service industry than a peer of this group. They'd call me when they needed me, but I was not really one of them. After my third drink I decide to move on. I find Leslie and Laurie in a tight clutch of women talking about the real estate market and say my good-byes. Noema is nowhere to be seen.

In my buzzed state, I decide I've had enough of these uppity chicks and stroll around the corner to the 12th St. Bar. The 12th St. Bar is deep in the gayborhood of Philly. Its entrance is on a piss-smelling alley backed up to a parking lot. It's seedy, it's divey, it's a perfect place to go if you don't want to be seen heading into a gay bar.

It's still early so I take my perch at the bar, a little overdressed but feeling 10 times more comfortable. I order my usual Jack and Coke and people watch. A lesbian couple is at the other end of the bar – they look like college girls, kind of scared but happily gazing into each other's eyes, keeping their hands on the other's knees. A pack of gay white boys just entered, loud and raucous. They head straight upstairs to the techno. I can hear it thumping and screeching all the way down here. I'm not a big fan of techno. An older black queen is holding down one of the booths in the back. She looks likes she's waiting for someone. I hope he shows up. I think about Candace. I wonder where she is and who she might have become. Is she somewhere hanging out in gay bars or she settled down with a partner; is she married to a man with children or is she alone? I hope she's not alone.... I hope she's happy, right?

As I start to wonder what I'm doing here at a bar, alone, on a Saturday night, I look across the room to the pool table in the back. A young black guy is playing pool with a woman around my age. I've seen her before at the clubs with her chocolate brown skin, short hair, and sly smiling eyes. She has on jeans, black motorcycle boots, and a white t-shirt with a black button-down over it. Her belt has a large Harley-Davison Belt buckle and there's a worn leather jacket lying on the couch next to her. I forget to be sad and pathetic for a while and just watch her. I take another sip of my drink and watch her slowly twirl a toothpick around in her mouth as she moves around the table. I look at the nape of her neck, I watch the bulge of her biceps, and I am mesmerized by the way she's expertly holding her cue stick.

I'm on my second drink when she finally notices me lusting after her. She lines up her ball, looks at me over the cue stick, and shoots. Ba-boom! The ball slams down and she smiles at me. I get a flutter in my stomach. She says something to her friend, puts down her stick, and walks straight over to me, never looking away. The flutter makes its way lower and lower.

"Hi. You like pool?" she asks. She's standing much too close to me. She puts her hand up on the bar. I'm caged in. Her hands look strong and I am suddenly weak. I try to regroup.

"No. I don't like pool all that much," I say. "I was mostly just watching you."

"Oh yeah? What's your name?" she asks, cutting to the chase.

"Dee. I'm Dee."

"I'm Angel." She leans forward and almost whispers in my ear, "Can I buy you a drink, Dee?" Her voice is like melted sugar, going all sticky and sweet. Her breath, warm on my neck, gives me goose bumps.

"Yes, sure, I'll have one more," I say, trying not to lose all common sense.

She orders us both drinks and sits on the stool next to mine. We toast. My drink burns a little, and my head swims.

"I like your shirt." she says. Her eyes are tracing my cleavage, her hands brushing my knees.

"Thanks," I say. "I like your belt." She puts her hand on her buckle. I try not to stare at her crotch. My mouth is suddenly dry.

"Do you ride?" she asks.

"No."

"Would you like to…take a ride?" she asks, her eyes looking mischievous.

"On a motorcycle? No, no thanks."

"Well, at least come and see it. It's big, it's black, it's shiny, and it's parked right out back." I'm shaking my head no, but I finish my drink. She caresses my hand and picks it up. She kisses my palm and I forget all my excuses. She coaxes me up, throws on her jacket and I follow her out the back exit. The door barely shuts behind me when she turns to me and kisses me. I kiss her back hard and she backs me onto the brick wall. Her hands are all over me while we kiss wildly. One hand is feeling my breast, the other is running up and down my thigh. I'm reaching around with my hand on the back of her head, the other around her waist. I can feel the hard brick on my back, my hair getting caught on its rough edges. She's got her tongue down my throat and I am throwing up one leg to bring her closer to me.

Somehow she frees my breast from my bra and she's got her fingers mashing my nipple. It feels like heaven. I slip my hand down to her neck and pull her head down, and she lifts my breast up and puts it in her mouth. As she sucks and licks me, her hand has moved in between my legs and she's rubbing me in circles. I'm trying to lick and bite her neck and unbutton my pants at the same time. I get them undone, she lifts her head back up to kiss me and plunges her hand in my pants, into my panties and finds my clit. I'm out here in the alley moaning under her stroking me, her other hand back on my nipple, her tongue in my mouth. I'm writhing under her and she presses her body against mine and grinds her hips on mine. I pull her closer and drag my fingers down her back. I'm breathing fast, I'm moaning louder, she puts her fingers inside me and fucks me hard and fast. Tongue, nipples, brick, fingers, leather, tongue, nipples, grinding, leather, brick, fucking, and I come, hard, shaking, yelling obscenities into her mouth. The waves of my orgasm break over and over, and she keeps her hand steady until they have subsided. My breathing slows and my clutch loosens. My haze starts to lift. Oh lord; did I just do what I think I did?

She pulls out her hand gently. I button up and tuck my breast back into its bra. She straightens her clothes, wipes her hand on her jeans, and clears her throat. I look around. I hear the sounds of the city but I don't see anybody else in this alley. She points.

"Um, here's my bike," she says and grins.

"Very cool," I manage to say.

"Sure you don't want a ride?" she asks.

"No, I think I'm gonna go." I step forward to kiss her good bye. "You were exquisite, amazing, god-like!" I grin. She grabs my hand.

"And you are very beautiful. Don't go yet. Stay. Let's have another drink. It's still early,".

"Yeah, it's early but I'm all wet now." I blush. "I gotta get home."

"Would you like some company?"

"No, thanks. I just want to be alone. Need to be alone, I think," I say.

"OK, darling. Well, if you want to hook up again, here's my card." I take it. We walk back in the bar. I continue through to the front entrance and she goes back to the pool table and her friend. It's around 11 p.m., the nights are not so cold, and more people are walking through the streets heading to their final destinations of the night. I walk to my car and get in. I look at the card. It reads 'Divine Detailing Heavenly Service for your Car by Angel'. I smile. I might hold on to this.

CHAPTER EIGHT

The next day, I go to my parent's house for dinner. I bring a salad and some red wine. My mom makes lasagna. My sister made a pound cake. After dinner my parents head into the living room to watch the NBA Playoffs and my sister and I stay in the kitchen with our wine.

"I went to go see Denise at the library," I say.

"Oh, how did that go?" Janine asks.

"Well, she still hates me, her whole family hates me and she will not give me any information about Candace nor pass any on. Dead end. But I have a new lead!"

"OK." Janine sips her wine and plays with the tablecloth.

I lower my voice and whisper, "I googled her!" She raises her eyebrows. "Nothing! But then I googled her best friend from high school and bingo! I have a hair appointment with her on Thursday!" My revelation does not get the reaction I was expecting.

"Shari? Dee, are you sure this is a good idea? Shari was a good friend of Candace's; she may not want to talk to you either. Maybe you should just leave well enough alone. I'm sure you're going to find a new girlfriend soon enough."

"Sis, can you be a little supportive? I want to find her. I need to find her," I say.

She sighs and looks frustrated. "Dee, what are you going to do if you find her? What if she has a husband and a family? Are you going to complicate all that for her?"

"No," I reply.

"Are you going to uproot your life, declare your love, and marry her?" she demands.

"Well…. No, I love my life here…." I start to say.

"Exactly! You are going to do what you always do, what *you* want to do, regardless of the consequences. I have seen you with many girlfriends who were all into you, but when you were done with them, you just left them high and dry and heart-broken." I'm stunned by her accusations but she continues on her rant. "And poor Pepper, she really loved you and you just dropped her out of the blue! For what? Because you started thinking about a girl from high school?"

"I didn't just drop her, I knew I wasn't in love with her and I just wanted…." I sound pathetic even to my own ears.

"It's only been two weeks and I bet you've already moved on . . . I bet you've already found someone else," she says looking at me intently.

I think back to the artist at the party last night, then to Angel in the alley and lower my eyes. "It was nothing," I protest.

"AHA! Seriously??? See! Heartbreaker! I love you, Dee, but sometimes you can be a player. Candace loved you. Despite everything that happened, we all could see that. You should leave her alone," she pleads.

I take a sip of my wine and feel abashed. Maybe I *should* just leave her alone. Am I really a heartbreaker? I hear my parents cheering in the next room.

"I'm gonna go check out the game," I say. Janine stays quiet and nods. I get up and leave her there. I can feel her eyes on my back.

CHAPTER NINE

My week at work turns out to be productive and satisfying. Meadow published her first article in *Midwifery Today Magazine*, and we celebrate with an office party. Soledad has found a midwife friend willing to care for her niece, so she is off the rampage. And I have two new patient appointments due to my networking on Saturday. It's one of those rare times when everything is going well and I am reminded of how lucky and blessed I am to actually enjoy my work. Off and on, I think about what my sister said to me. I start to have doubts about myself but I have the hair appointment and I need to get my hair done. So at the very least, I'm going to see Shari.

Thursday rolls around and I'm nervous. Shari was the girl who took the bus with Candace every day to and from school. She was her oldest friend, her best friend until I came along. We never had too much to say to each other, but I know how devoted she was to Candace.

I pull up to the salon and am immediately impressed. It's a clean, well-kept looking storefront with very upscale looking signage. I walk in, a bell softly tinkles, and a young but very courteous receptionist greets me.

"Good afternoon, how may I help you?" she says. I'm taken aback. Am I in Philly? We never get this kind of good treatment from our own.

"Good afternoon," I reply. "I'm here for my 3:30 p.m. appointment with Shari."

"OK. Please have a seat in our waiting area. There is fresh lemon water and fruit for your enjoyment while you wait," she says.

What the hell? Seriously, am I still in Philly? Even if this Candace thing does not work out, this is my new salon. I take a seat on the velvet chaise lounge and help myself to a couple of strawberries and grapes. Not two minutes later is my name called and I follow the receptionist to the Beauty Area.

I have a seat in the chair and Shari walks out to greet me. She looks much the same as she did in high school, maybe a little rounder and with more grace and confidence. She's dressed impeccably in a cream-colored cotton knit wrap dress. When she sees me, she does a double take and a range of emotions flash across her face. She's clearly surprised, but she's a professional and this is her place of business.

She approaches me with a tight smile and exclaims, "Deirdre! My goodness. It's good to see you! I haven't seen you since we graduated high school!" She gives me a perfunctory hug. The clients and stylists around us smile and nod approvingly. They love this place; it's so full of good vibes and peacefulness.

"Shari! Oh my God! Is this your place? It's fabulous! I was looking for a new place to get my hair done when I drove pass one day. I just had to try it out," I lie. She smiles and turns me around in the chair so we both can see in the mirror.

"Great! I'm so glad you did. So what are you having done today, Deirdre? I love this style on you, I love the natural look," she exclaims.

"Just a good wash, condition, and a cut. My ends are getting raggedy. It's been a while since I've been to a salon, as you can probably tell. And please, call me Dee," I say.

I knew she resented my friendship with Candace, but I didn't know how much until she sighed, shook her head and said, "Listen, Dee, I can't…. You know what? I'm going to turn you over to my best stylist in here. I forgot, but I just have something really important to do."

She backed away from me and went into a back room. A few minutes later, another woman came out and did my hair. I kept hearing my sister's words – "heartbreaker, heartbreaker" – over and over again. The woman finished my hair; she was gentle, kind and good. I looked great. I felt conflicted. I paid and tipped and then asked to see Shari.

For several long minutes, I waited. I started to think that this was a lost cause; she clearly still resented me and wanted to have nothing to do with me. Finally, she came out with her jacket on and gestured for me to follow her. We walked out of the shop and around the corner to a park bench.

"What do you want, Dee?" she asks.

"I want to find Candace," I say. She is quiet. I continue. "I haven't seen her since graduation and the other day, I was looking at old photo albums and I thought of her and I was just wondering whatever became of her," I lie. I was getting way too comfortable with lying.

"If you and Candace aren't friends anymore, that's between you two. I love and trust Candace, and if she cut you off, I'm sure she had a good reason for doing it," she says. I realized then that she had no idea about the extent of my relationship with Candace. We had been very good at subterfuge.

"So, you are still in touch with her? How is she? What's she doing?" I ask desperately. I feel so close to getting answers, but the look on Shari's face is stony.

"Look, Candace and I have been friends for a long time – twenty years, as a matter of fact. The only time we ever had issues was when you came along. Then she just cut me off. One day we were best friends, the next day, my best friend was gone, busy and everything was different. And yes, I blame you. I'm over it now, of course, but it hurt me a lot back then ... a lot." She paused, and then continued.

"After graduation, she and I went down to Spelman like we had always planned and it was all good again. She never once mentioned you. We're grown, she and I are still friends, and I don't see where you fit into the picture, not then, not now."

I have three options. Number one, I could just beg her to pass along my information and hope that Candace gets back to me, but this seemed highly unlikely. Number two, I could lie and make up some tragedy to try to get her sympathy and maybe she would help me. This also seemed unlikely, and I did not want to finally find Candace and then immediately have to admit to a lie. Number three, I could confess my love for Candace and hope that she would understand and have some kind of romantic bone in her body. This also seemed like a long shot.

I look at Shari. She is getting impatient. I notice her wedding ring and think back to the gentleness and peacefulness of her shop full of women being meticulously cared for. I plunge ahead with number three, hoping that love will conquer all.

"Shari," I begin cautiously, "I know you don't know me now and didn't know me much then, but I'm not the bad person you think I am. In high school, I fell in love with Candace. She was my first love and I loved her with all my heart. Things did not work out between us, obviously, but I never meant her any harm, not then and not now. I just want to see her again, make sure that she is happy." As this is coming out of my mouth, I see her processing, making connections, and becoming disgusted all at the same time. It's an interesting look but not an encouraging one.

"Dee, I heard all those rumors at school and I sincerely hope that you did not try to bring Candace into any of that nastiness. It certainly would explain why Candace rejected you. My husband is a pastor and we'll pray for you. But I don't want you to have anything to do with my girl, Candace," she says emphatically. "Now, I have to get back to work. Have a nice life." And with that she left.

I probably should have gone with the lie. Depressed, I walk slowly back to my car, passing by the salon one more time. I guess I won't be getting my hair done there either. Doubly disappointed, I get in my car and drive off.

I end up on Olney Avenue and decide to park my car outside of Girls' High. There's not too much activity there now; school has been out for a couple of hours. But a few girls go by with instruments, leaving band practice or maybe orchestra. How could Shari not know or even guess about us? How could Candace never tell her anything? Maybe I'm making a big mistake. Maybe the whole love affair was blown up and exaggerated in my mind. Maybe it didn't mean the quite the same for her.

Candace and I were together through the winter and spring of our sophomore year. That summer, however, we were apart. I spent my summer working as a candy striper at a local hospital and watching my little sister and her friends. I also discovered feminism that summer and started reading more books by women, about women.

Candace always went to her grandmother's house in South Carolina for the month of July; that year was no different. In August, she spent the first two weeks at her Dad's house in Chicago; her mom monopolized the second two. We wrote letters and cards to each other and talked on the phone a lot. But we were used to seeing each other just about every day and it was hard to be apart.

When we finally did get a chance to hang out a few days before school started back up, we went to Blue Bell Park, a small, little used park in West Mount Airy. Getting off the bus and walking up the entranceway, we were quiet. I was nervous to see her again. It had been two months since we were physically in the same place. I wasn't sure if things would be the same. We had chatted on the bus, but now we would get a chance to be alone. She was a little taller, a little leaner; her face looked more like a woman's face than a girl's. I had stopped straightening my hair and cut it shorter. I wondered if she hated it. Passing the parking lot we went to our favorite tree, a tall, vast oak tree that leaned heavily to the right. We sat under it, cross-legged, and looked at each other. I looked around; we were alone. I took her hands in mine. She sighed.

"Hi," I said.

"Hi," she replied, "I missed you. I missed seeing your face everyday." She reached out to touch my hair. "Natural, huh? I think I like it. Of course, you got that good hair so you can get away with it," she teased.

"Shut up. You are still so beautiful. Even more, I think. Hey, you got a second hole in your ear!" I leaned in. She had a weird-looking post earring in there. "What's that?"

"It's a lambda." Then she whispered, "It's a gay symbol, but only gay people know about it."

"Ohhhh. Cool. Where did you learn about that?" I asked.

"In Chicago. I learned some interesting things in Chicago," she said mysteriously.

"From who?" I felt a twinge of jealousy.

"From someone I met there," she answered, batting her eyes. I didn't think this was funny at all.

"Who?" I said a little too harshly, pulling my hands away.

"Oh, relax," she said. "My dad's next-door neighbor is this flaming queen named Pierre. He is super-gay, but he's a fashion designer so nobody cares. I went in his apartment and saw all kinds of crazy stuff. And he talked, a lot!"

Relieved, I asked, "Did you tell him about us?"

"No! I just listened to him. I saw this symbol one day, and asked him about it. A few days later, I was downtown shopping and I saw it, so I bought it. I was thinking about you, you know." She grabbed my hands back and held them. "Were you thinking about me?" she asked, looking a little uncertain of herself.

I smiled and said, "Every moment of every day." We looked around, leaned forward and kissed. Nothing had changed between us.

Our junior year began and we were more mature, more confident in our feelings for each other, but still very cautious and careful to make sure we were never found out, which is why I was stunned when, in October, a girl I hardly knew, a girl I'd only had one class with, Vivian Dupree, whispered in my ear one day, "I know about you."

I spun around and looked her dead in the eye, and stuttered, "You don't know anything about me!" and I stalked off. I could hear her laughter behind me. "Oh yes, I do!" I kept walking.

That night, I called Candace in a panic and told her what happened.

"Oh no! Well, wait, maybe she's talking about something else. She has to be. How could she possibly know? We're fine!" She tried to reassure me, but I could hear the uncertainty in her voice.

"There's nothing else to know about me, Candace! I'm boring; I have no drama except for that argument in Spanish club last week, which was stupid anyway. There's nothing to know!"

I was terrified. My school had shown no new signs of tolerance and in fact was caught up in being super-feminine after some ridiculous criticisms written in the school paper. Even I had caved and worn a skirt to school that week.

"OK, let's think. Do you have any classes with her?"

"Not this year."

"Are you in any clubs with her or any of her friends?

"Not that I know of. I don't even think she has friends, I never see her with anybody."

"Maybe she's just making a joke, or trying to get you upset for some reason. I'm sure it's something stupid. Nobody knows how much I love you, nobody, except you." We giggled, but I was still uneasy.

I did not see Vivian for the rest of the week, but spent it looking over my shoulder anyway. That weekend, on a warm and sunny Saturday, Candace and I went back to Blue Bell Park. Instead of stopping at our favorite tree, we walked past the fields and into the woods. We made out behind a row of fir trees. It smelled so good back there. Clean and fresh but cozy too. We had finally graduated from just kissing to kissing and touching. The first time I put my hand up to cup her breast, I just about died from embarrassment. I felt like such a boy, an inexperienced boy at that. But she grabbed my hand and kept it there. It was the first time I had touched a breast that wasn't mine. She was fuller than me, rounder. The next time there, she lowered her hands from my back to my ass. I jumped, but she just laughed and reached up to hold my breast as well. This particular day we were making out pretty fast and furious, leaving each other breathless and yearning.

Suddenly, I heard a CRACK! We froze. I yanked down my shirt. We stepped away from each other and looked around. It was quiet. Then we heard a rustling further away, but the sound was fading. We stepped out of the woods and I saw the back of a girl walking a dog. I knew that Jeff cap. We looked around; nobody else was there. But our passion was extinguished for the day and we hurried home.

Monday morning before classes started, I saw Vivian by her locker. She had on that same Jeff cap. I went up to her and said, "Can I talk to you … in private?" She looked at me and laughed.

"Sure," she said. We found an empty art room and went inside.

Confidently I began, "I don't know what you think you saw, but you didn't see anything."

"I have no idea what you're talking about, Dee," she replied.

"You know what I'm talking about, and I'm telling you, you didn't see anything!" I said.

"No, I didn't see anything…nothing at all, except you and your girlfriend making out." She grinned at me very satisfied with herself.

"Sshhhhh!! Vivian, I was not making out with anybody, I don't know what you're talking about. Please…." I pleaded.

"Relax," she said. "I'm not going to tell anybody. Your secret is safe with me…as long as mine is safe with you." She smiled. I looked at her wondering whether to trust her or not.

"You?" I said. She nodded and raised her eyebrows.

"Me. Me, too, that is," she said. She tucked her hair behind her ear and I saw a tiny lambda symbol in her fourth hole. I was shocked. Then I was happy and I laughed.

"You won't tell anybody, will you? Seriously, we don't want anybody to know," I said.

"Of course not! And vise versa. Deal?" She stuck out her hand.

I shook it and said, "Deal!" And after that we were friends.

It was awkward in the beginning, as we didn't really have anything in common but our interest in girls, and for me really just one girl. Candace was a little suspicious of our friendship at first, but she got over it. It ended up being educational for both of us since Viv had been "in the life" a year longer than us. And Viv, while very outgoing and assertive at school, was nevertheless skilled in the ways of deception about her private life. It took me two months to learn that her "friend" lived in her neighborhood but went to Creative and Performing Arts. They'd only been together a few months but it was Viv's second relationship. The first had been with an older girl on her neighborhood basketball team.

I think Viv saw me as a pet project/ little sister. But for me, she was my entrée into a world I had no idea existed. She gossiped about celebrities, athletes, and teachers. I had been so caught up in my own love affair that I hadn't really thought much about who else might also like other girls. As far as I knew, Candace and I (and Celie and Shug, of course) were the only girls who felt this way. Candace was my first gay love, but Viv was my gay tour guide. I was truly happy and relieved to have an experienced friend who I could be honest with, who I could hang out with, and who could answer my many gay questions.

Viv! I shake myself out of my reverie. Why hadn't I thought of Vivian before? She'll help me find Candace. She, more than anyone else, knows what Candace meant to me. But, man, I haven't talked to Vivian in a really long time. We lost touch through my college years but then re-connected when I came home to Philadelphia. But soon after that, she moved to Brooklyn with her new girlfriend. I start my car and get moving. Her contact info is somewhere in a card in my pile of things to do.

➥ CHAPTER TEN ➦

At home, I admire my new hair in the mirror. Damn, she did do a good job. Ah well, *c'est la vie*. I grab a glass of water and look at the pile. It's almost a foot tall and I know I will get distracted. Everything in that pile is something I should have filed, followed up on, looked up, or replied to in a timely manner. That pile is full of annoying details that I am totally not interested in right now, and it is way too much. I turn on the TV and watch the evening news instead. Then I make myself a sandwich with a salad. I eyeball the pile. Then I clean up and have a glass of white wine. I walk by and touch the pile. Then I check my email. I glance at the pile. OK, all right already. I pick up the paper on top. Right, I have to make my dental appointment! Ugh!

Two hours later I finally make it to the birthday card Viv sent me last year. It's got a cute little kitten on the front with a Happy Birthday ribbon around its neck. On the inside Viv wrote, "Thought I'd send you a little something in case you ain't getting any lately!!!" At the bottom she put her new address and phone number. The trick will be if she is still with this girlfriend and hasn't already moved out.

I call the number but just get the voice mail. At least it's her voice. I tell her to call me back; I've got a life or death mission for her. In the pile I also find the business card from Noema, Leslie and Laurie's artist friend. The card has an interesting design; it reminds me of the bit of tattoo I saw on her neck. Should I? Shouldn't I? I'm supposed to be looking for my lost love, right? I should take a break from dating, right? Of course, I should. I put the card back in the pile and go to bed.

BBBBRrrrriingg! I bolt upright in bed! It's 3:17am, must be Ananda and Anil. I answer the phone.

"Aarrrargh! Dee? It's time!"

I smile. I love my job. I reassure my patient, get the information I need, get dressed, grab my bag, and go.

⁂

Friday night, I get home and crash. It was a good labor, but the delivery was tricky. Four hours of coaxing and calling this little boy forward. But when he arrived he was just gorgeous, and did he have a set of lungs on him! I had to admit Ananda to the hospital after the birth, but I'm so glad we were able to have the baby just like she wanted to, on her terms. I wake up late Saturday morning and get ready to go see her when I notice the blinking light on my phone. I check my messages and it's Vivian. Excellent. I call her back immediately.

"Hey, stranger!" She sounds like she's still in bed under the covers.

"Hey, Viv! How're you doing? I've been thinking about you!" I say excitedly.

" Oh yeah? And just what have you been thinking? And what is this secret mission you mentioned? You know I like a mystery," she says.

"OK, I haven't talked to you in a year, but I guess we can dispense with the catching up," I surmise. "Well, since you ask. I know you might think its stupid, or a bad idea but … I'm looking for Candace. I thought you might be able to help me find her," I say. She laughs, of course.

"Looking for Candace?" she exclaims. "Why, Dee darling, after all these years would you go looking for her?" she asks.

Sigh. "Viv, now don't laugh again, but I was just thinking ... a lot of things have been happening lately and I.... You know I never loved anybody like I loved her, and I just want to know." I struggle to get it out.

"Dee, I know how much you loved her, but we were just kids then. Your first love will always mean a lot to you, but it doesn't mean you can go back there. You're just being nostalgic. What? Did you just have a break-up or something?" she asks.

"Well, yes," I reply, "but that doesn't really have anything to do with it. I realized that I was just not in love with Pepper...."

"Pepper!" she hollered. "You were dating a stripper?" She laughs.

"Funny. No, that was…is just her name. Whatever! Anyway, I realized that I wasn't in love with her, and I was thinking and I couldn't really honestly say that I've been with anybody who I was totally in love with ... except Candace," I say.

"So what? Are you finally looking to settle down or something? Maybe you just haven't met the right person yet," she argues.

"Maybe the right person was Candace, but we were just too young back then," I insist.

"Oh, for heaven's sake, Dee! Are you serious?" she asks.

"Serious as a heart attack," I reply. She sighs and I can imagine her rolling her eyes.

"OK, well, this should be interesting. How can I help you?" she relents.

"Well, I tried but her family still will not talk to me. Neither will her friend, Shari, remember her? She knows where she is but won't tell me. Don't you have a cousin that went down to Morehouse the same time we graduated? I think I remember that he, Brian, I think, and Candace were friends. Maybe they stayed friends or maybe he knows somebody who knows her. Can you ask him? For me? Please?" I say.

"OK," Viv says, "but for the record, I think you are setting yourself up for disappointment."

"Duly noted, but thank you!" I say.

"It might take me a while, I haven't talked to Brian in years," she says.

"That's OK, any help would be great. I hate to ask a favor and run, but I've got to get to a patient," I say.

"No problem. I'll let you know when I talk to Brian," she says.

"Thanks Viv. I owe you one," I say.

"Oh, you owe me several, and one day you'll pay up, just you wait!" she exclaims.

We hang up. I look at the clock and run out the door praying for no traffic.

☙ CHAPTER ELEVEN ❧

I manage to stay out of trouble all weekend, but when I walk into work on Monday morning, trouble is there waiting for me ... Pepper. Stepping out of her car, right outside my job, where I work. Pepper is looking angry. Pepper is looking upset. Pepper is looking like trouble way too early on a Monday morning.

I sneak a peek at my watch. My first patient, a new patient, does not come for another 45 minutes. I hope I can get through this by then. I walk over to her calmly.

"Hi, Pepper. What's up?" I ask casually but firmly. I want to stay in control of this situation.

"What's up?" She repeats. "That's what you have to say to me? What's up? Like we're just friends, like you don't know how much you've hurt me?" Uh-oh. I look around.

"Would you like to go somewhere and talk? I don't really want to talk here outside my office, OK?" I suggest.

"I'm not moving anywhere." She plants her hands on her hips and lays into me, right there in the middle of the street. "I'm gonna say what I have to say and then I am done. A month has gone by and I have been stupidly waiting for you to realize what an asinine mistake you've made. I've been waiting for a phone call, a visit, an email, something, anything that would make me think that you ever cared about me at all. But nothing."

"Pepper," I say, "I'm sorry. I didn't mean to hurt you, I ..." She holds up her hand for silence. I close my mouth.

Pepper continues loudly, "We were together for six months, six good months, at least I thought so until you broke up with me for some bullshit reason. I just want to know, for me, for my sanity, did I ever mean anything to you?"

I hesitate. I don't know what to say. Honestly, I have not thought about her much since we broke up. Did she mean anything to me?

"Pepper, I don't have to tell you this, but you are a good person – smart, caring, and at times, quite a force to be reckoned with. I loved the time we spent together, but I never planned on it being anything serious. And I just felt we had reached our peak and it was time to move on. It's nothing personal against you, it was just time for me. I'm sorry you are hurt. I really am ... that was never my intention." I hold my ground. I had spoken the truth. She knew it.

"OK, Dee, thank you. Now I know that it wasn't me, it was you. You're the asshole. Thanks." She sniffs and gets back into her car. Her eyes well up with tears and she drives away. I stand there wondering if I should have lied or mentioned Candace, but I think not. Maybe I am an asshole, an unfeeling, self-centered asshole. At least I'm an honest asshole, I reason, but I doubt that'll be any consolation for her.

I watch her drive off, and then I turn and walk into the office. Tracy Ann discreetly greets me as if she hadn't been watching and listening to the whole thing.

"Here are your messages and here's your schedule for the day," she says brightly. "Your first appointment should be here any minute." I get the hint and rush back to my office to prepare.

I spend the rest of the week immersed in work. I meet two new patients, prepare Amanda and Josh as they enter their third trimester, deliver a beautiful baby girl, attend an all-day CNM professional development workshop and we have our monthly administrative meeting.

Friday morning, after my last patient of the day leaves, I check my voice messages. I have one from Bernie's little sister.

"Hey, Dee! It's Beverly! Just wanted to let you know that we are going to have a fitting for the bridesmaids' gowns next Friday, around 6 p.m. I'll text you the shop. Also, the wedding itself will be the first weekend in October, so plan for the bachelorette party to be Labor Day weekend. I'll let you know about the bridal shower, but it'll be sometime in the summer, OK? Can't wait to see you. Toodles!"

Furiously writing all the dates down I think, ugh, I have totally forgotten about Bernie's wedding! Bridesmaid gown. Oh lawd, but do I hate those two words! I call Vivian but just get her voicemail; I leave her a message but am not feeling optimistic. Viv can be flaky.

Friday night, I try another internet search to find Candace, but I can't find anything new. I don't even know what kind of career she could have. In high school she talked about being a lawyer, but a lot of people did. She might have a married name. I hadn't thought about that before. I open a bottle of shiraz, pull out a book, and try not to feel too lonely.

Sunday night, I finally hear back from Viv. I'm just getting home from dinner with my parents and ever so judgmental sister when my cell rings. It's a warm night so I sit on my balcony to talk.

"Viv! I've been waiting for you to call." I cringe. I sound like Pepper the other day.

"Hey, girl! Sorry, but I had a super busy week and then the wife was acting up and then the cat got sick, you know how it is. Stupid cat cost me $175 at the vet. It's not even my cat!" complains Viv.

"Sorry about your cat, Viv. So ... did you get a chance to talk to your cousin?" I ask anxiously. I'm trying not to be impatient but I'm impatient!!!

"Oh, Brian! Yes, I talked to him on Tuesday. He does remember Candace from college."

"Tuesday!!! Why didn't you call me on Tuesday?" I ask, exasperated.

"I said I was having wife and cat issues. That trumps your finding lost love issue any day," she replies.

Sighing, I ask, "OK, so does he have any ideas about how to find her? Or where she might have gone? Maybe she's still in Atlanta," I offer hopefully.

"Well, good news and bad news, or it could be good news depending on how you look at it."

"Spit it out, Viv!" I say.

"OK, well, for most of their time down there, Brian remembers Candace having a boyfriend named Kevin. He said it had to be for at least three years. He said they were always together. Now, he has no idea what happened to Candace, but he's certain that Kevin still lives in Atlanta. He took over his father's bar. That's the good news."

"That's your idea of good news? That she had a boyfriend for three years?" I ask.

"Yes," she replies. "The bad news is that this guy is somewhat of a recluse. He runs his bar but is hard to get a hold of. Brian thinks if we want to talk to him, we'll have to go down there and speak to him in person."

"Fly down to Atlanta just to ask someone a question? What's good about that?" I ask.

She laughs and roars, "ROADTRIP!!!"

The end of May, with its beautiful weather, has finally shown up like a fairy godmother, bestowing blessings of warmth and flowers and smiles and goodwill. The rest of the week is busy. I'm on the phone with Viv about dates and times and airplane tickets and hotels. We finally settle on going the following weekend. I'm excited. It's been a year since I've gone anywhere and even longer since I spent time with my long lost friend. And of course, I might find Candace.

On Thursday morning, Laurie and Leslie come in for their fifth month appointment. Laurie gives me a big squeeze hello so I get a good feel of that baby inside her rounding her out, making her cheeks even rosier, her dimples even deeper. Leslie comes in wearing a black tank top and cargo pants. I try my best to keep focused on Laurie, but Leslie keeps talking to me. Finally she asks me the question that must have been on her mind since she walked in the door.

"So, have you contacted Noema, yet?" she asks casually, her face looking anything but indifferent.

"Oh no, not yet. I meant to give her a call. I just got busy here at work and with some other things, you know." I try to be breezy about it.

"Oh sure, I bet it can get real busy here. Well, she did ask me to tell you hello when we saw you today. We almost brought her with us, but she had a meeting with a gallery owner. She's going to be the baby's godmother, you know," Leslie says.

All of a sudden it's clear to me what this fantasy is about. Hooking up their baby's midwife and their baby's godmother would be like creating a trifecta of love and positive energy surrounding their little family. Oh brother. Still, that Noema had something about her and I'm really curious about that tattoo.

"I'll give her a call, soon. I promise," I say. "Now Laurie, could you open up a little bit wider? This is going to be a little chilly…."

Friday at 5 p.m. I get the text about the bridal shop. I try to get myself psyched up, but I don't know many of Bernie's other friends and her sister will definitely wear me out. I drive out to the Main Line and get there just a little bit late. The shop is fairly large with three separate lounge areas for different bridal parties. I'm pleasantly surprised. Its not super expensive Main Line upper crusty, but it's classy and stylish, modern with some cool. Six women are milling about a small table with wine and crudités. Bernie is among them, but she looks stressed.

"Hey, Dee. Glad you could make it." She's wringing her hands.

"Sure! What's the matter, Bernie? You look a wreck." I hug her.

"My sister and mother are trying to sabotage my wedding, that's what!" she whispers, handing me a glass of wine. "Every time I tell them what I want, they arrange for the opposite. Every time I try to have some input, they blow me off. I had to fight to use this bridal store. They wanted something even more traditional! I'm about to lose my mind, but wait until you see my dress. It's perfect!"

"I'm sure everything will work out. Just stick to your guns. It's your big day. Right?" I try to reassure her, but I'm sure those two witches are riding her hard. She's always been the golden girl of the family and everyone has hitched their wagon to her star. As she starts to introduce me around, her mom and sister blow in the door like dual tornadoes of demands and bossiness.

Her mother starts in first. "Bernadette! You are not in your dress yet?? What are you waiting for a personal invitation? For God's sake, that's what we are all here for!" she cries.

Beverly has already taken the store attendant aside and is scolding her about the wine selection and the tardiness of the dress selections. It's going to be a long night. I look at Bernadette, her lips are tightly pressed together as she holds her tongue, but it's just a matter of time before this situation blows up.

Her other bridesmaids include her best friend from high school, a mentor from medical school, Darryl's two sisters, and one of the other doctors in her practice. They all seem nice and we look at and discuss the bridesmaids' selection. We agree to a hot little cocktail wrap dress with a pale unassuming print. We all look good in it and could possibly wear it again, which is fortunate since it costs $300.

After admiring ourselves in the various mirrors, we are instantly humbled when Bernie steps out of the dressing room. Like some kind of African goddess, her locks are piled high and spilling down her open back. The dress is off-white, but long and slim with a slight train. No worries, we are definitely the back-up singers in this scenario. I don't remember her ever looking so gorgeous and regal. I suppress the urge to bow.

"Bernie, I'm in awe. Truly, you look spectacular," I say sincerely.

"Thanks, I hope Darryl thinks so, too. He deserves the best and I aim to give him just that." Looking at me, she adds, "I know it's not your thing, but I hope you fall in love one day, Dee. It might just be really good for you, you never know. In any event, please bring a date, OK?"

I open my mouth to reply, but her mother comes rushing over to fuss and fret over the low cut back. I close my mouth. 'Not my thing?' Is that what she really thinks? Why would she think that? But I don't get a chance to ask her. Beverly is on a schedule and we need to get measured and put down our deposits. I do what's required, but feel unsettled the rest of the night.

The weekend passes quickly. One of my patients goes into labor early Saturday morning and delivers a healthy baby boy late Sunday night. It's a challenging delivery, so I stay at the birth center the whole weekend. By Monday afternoon, I am exhausted and finally head home for a decent shower and some sleep. The rest of the week is a blur as I try to squeeze in all my appointments and hand off my third trimester patients' information to Meadow and Soledad. I want to go to Hotlanta without worrying about their care.

❧ CHAPTER TWELVE ❧

Friday morning, I finish packing my five outfits – two just in case we find Candace and I have to look good, one a more formal look, the other, casual and cute, one traveling comfy outfit, one going to the club outfit, and one basic look that I could get away with anywhere. I throw on some Jill Scott as I drive up the NJ Turnpike to the Newark airport. She always calms my nerves.

It's only when I started driving that I began to imagine what it will be like to see Candace again. What if this guy gives us her address? Will we just show up at her door? What if he gives us her phone number? Am I just going to call her? Maybe he will arrange a meeting at some random place? That seems so unlikely. The more I speculate, the more unsure I feel about the whole thing. I wonder what she looks like now. I check my face in the rearview mirror. I hope I haven't aged too much.

After parking, check-in and security, I head up to the gate. I see Vivian before she sees me. She still looks fabulous, of course. She's wearing tight jeans and a simple white t-shirt with some kind of blingy design on the front. She's standing in red open-toe short boots with heels. Her hair is shorter than it used to be, its kind of a bob – casual but chic. Of course, she's wearing sunglasses, and I can see the glint of her glossy plum lipstick from here.

I look down wishing I had on something more impressive than my Georgetown University hoodie and black sweatpants. I like to be comfortable when I travel, but I quickly surmise that I will be mistaken for Viv's personal assistant if I don't up my game. I contemplate running into the restroom to at least throw on some make-up, but Viv turns and sees me. She laughs her 'Viv laugh' and strides on over to me, arms thrown wide. She has to bend down to hug me because of those ridiculous heels.

" Deeeeeeeee!!! I've missed you so much!" she cries, laughing heartily and giving me a bear hug.

"Viv! You look great—it's so good to see you!!!" I reply, squeezing her back. "Thanks for coming with me, Viv. And thanks for helping me find her."

"Oh, I wouldn't miss this for the world!" she laughs.

I grab my bag and we walk straight to Cinnabon. It's an old habit of ours. In high school, we'd hit the Cinnabon in the mall when we took road trips to New York City or DC. In our twenties, we stopped at the rest stops just for the Cinnabon, and the one time we flew together to LA, we visited Cinnabon at every layover. We had just gotten our buns when our flight was called. It was going to be perfect for the short flight. We stowed our bags and sat down. I take the window seat—I love watching the clouds. Viv takes the aisle, better for her long legs and better to be seen. We chat about small things, the weather, traffic, the length of the flight, the hotel where we are staying. Then the plane taxis and my favorite part of flying begins – take-off.

We speed down the runway, faster and faster, my heart keeping time, and then we pull up against gravity, pull up away from earth and strain towards the sky. The rumble of the engines, the roar of the wind against the plane, a demonstration of power, proving that we humans can get away if we want to, can leave the constraints of what we know and what we have to do and our daily lives to fly in the sky above the clouds, above the birds and across the land and oceans. I love takeoff. It's short but it makes me feel free.

Viv is watching me, grinning. I've already waxed poetic about take-off to her. She finds me amusing. I know it. It doesn't bother me. I find her a little over the top. She knows it and I think she exaggerates it just for me. We maintain the friendship we started in high school and it suits us just fine.

"So," she begins, "what is this all about, really?" Just like her to cut through the bullshit.

"I think I'm ready to settle down. I want to have somebody, I want to be in love." I have nothing to hide with her.

"And you think you want to settle down with Candace?" she asks.

"I don't know," I shrug.

"You know you haven't seen her in 15 years. She might have changed. You've changed some, not a lot, but you've grown up. Don't you think she has too?" she asks.

"I'm sure she has. But Viv, I have had at least 10 girlfriends since then, women I was serious about, who I liked a lot, who I loved, but I have never felt like any of them were 'right' for me. I never wanted to stay with them or marry them. There was always something missing."

"What about Nia? I thought you two were made for each other. You were together for a year. I thought that was pretty serious," she says.

"It was, and even though we got along great, I never burned for her, you know? I never was just insanely head over heels in love with her. I loved her but it was not the same...."

"Maybe it just wasn't the right time for you and Nia. You know, Dee, when you were with Candace, we were in high school and we were all hormonal and dramatic teenagers, right? Your first love is your first love. I don't think anything ever compares to that, but I don't think it's possible to really get it back, Dee," she says gently.

"Maybe," I say. "But I just have to know. I have to know. My feelings for her, my love for her never really went away. I just, I just want to at least see her again," I say, feeling the emotion rising in my chest. Viv looks at me like I'm a lost cause.

"OK! Well, hopefully we'll find her. And if nothing else, road trip!!!" she exclaims excitedly. I smile at her and watch her pull out a celebrity gossip magazine and tear into her Cinnabon. I look out the window and think about Candace.

After I started hanging around with Vivian, my relationship with Candace got even stronger. Now that I had a friend who I could be honest with, it became clearer to me how I could still be just good friends with a girl and that it was completely different from being in love with one. I was having a really good year. I turned 16 that November and started learning how to drive. I could not wait to be able to pick Candace up in my mom's car and take her somewhere on a real date.

Christmas came and I felt like I didn't need a thing. I was truly happy with life. Christmas night, I went over to Candace's house so we could exchange gifts. I had bought her a gold chain with a tiny amethyst pendant. She bought me a purple hat, a scarf and gloves set, and a journal and pen with purple ink. We sneaked a kiss in the kitchen then went out to eat cookies and watch a movie with her mom and sisters. We sat together on the couch, the Christmas tree lights reflected in the TV screen where I had my first taste of spiked eggnog courtesy of Denise, and fell happily asleep.

The next day, I was sitting around with my mom, looking over our gifts and listening to Johnny Mathis sing when she gave me some great news.

"Dee," she said, "Your father and I are gonna go to Atlantic City for New Year's Eve this year. And your sister has been invited over to her friend Stacey's house. That leaves you. You are old enough to stay home by yourself, but why don't you invite one of your friends over to hang out here? They could spend the night, and then I wouldn't be worried about you being here by yourself." I tried to appear calm and collected.

"Hmmm, OK. Maybe I'll invite Candace or Vivian over. I'm not sure what they are doing. Atlantic City, huh? Sounds like you and Dad are gonna have some fun!" I said. Inside I was jumping up and down, turning cartwheels and shouting 'Hallelujah!!!' Five long minutes later, I excused myself and called Candace from my bedroom with the door closed.

"Hi! It's me. I have the best news ever!! My parents are going away for New Years, my sister is going away for New Years and I'll be here alone. My mom *wants* me to invite a friend over. Would you like to come over and spend New Years Eve with me?' I asked dramatically.

"Oh my God!!! Yes!! OK, I've got to ask my mom but I'm sure she'll say yes. Oh, I can't wait! Nobody will be there? Dee, do you know what this means?" she asked.

"Yes, we can finally have some privacy, we can sleep in the same...Candace...we can...." I trailed off nervously, my mouth suddenly dry.

"Yup. Dee, do you think we're ready? Are you ready?" she asked quietly.

"Wow, OK. I think so. I love you Candace. You know that, right?" I said.

"I know. I love you too. I'm ready," she said.

"OK, me too! OK, go ask your mom and call me right back!"

New Year's Eve came and I was a nervous wreck. I tried very hard to appear normal but I was a mess. Thankfully, nobody noticed. My mother was busy cooking her black-eyed peas, collard greens, and rice. My sister was getting ready for her sleepover and my father was out getting his car detailed. He likes a clean car for the new year. I, uncharacteristically, cleaned my room and the bathroom. I changed my sheets and towels and changed my clothes five times. I changed my underwear three times. No, four.

Of course, I had already consulted with Viv; she was excited for me and insisted that I borrow her VCR copy of a lesbian film, *Desert Hearts*, and her Tracy Chapman tape. I had already made my own "love" mix tape and had my boombox set up by my bed. I felt weird with all this planning, but it was a once in a lifetime opportunity and I didn't want to waste it. Viv also wanted to give me some sex tips, but I didn't want to talk about the actual "act" too much. It was too embarrassing. I wanted my first time to be between Candace and me. I really didn't want Viv to be a part of it, no matter how good a friend she was. Of course, I listened to her pep talk and offers of practice (no thanks!) but I decided to wing it and hoped I knew enough about sex to get it right. That day, I must have talked to Candace six times, but each time we just updated each other on what we were doing and we giggled a lot.

My mom finished cooking and we had a small family meal around 5 p.m. I ate a little but my stomach was in knots. Then my parents got dressed and left with my sister around 7 p.m. Candace was being dropped off by her family around 8 p.m. on their way to a church service. In the hour between, I paced the house, listened to the radio and re-arranged my room. I might have changed my underwear again. I was pre-occupied with "freshness."

When the bell rang, I jumped. I opened the door and let Candace in, and we waved to her family and watched them drive off. We went into the house and closed the door. I took her coat; she thanked me. We were awkward. I offered her something to eat, but she wasn't hungry. I asked her what was in her bag, but she wasn't ready to show me. We laughed at our "weirdness" but that didn't put an end to it.

I turned up the music; we danced, tentative at first. It was the first time we'd really danced together. We were bound to the house but I'd never felt so free. Michael Jackson came on and we danced ourselves out until they went to commercial.

I showed her Viv's movie, and she seemed excited to see it. So I turned off the radio, made popcorn and we settled on the couch to watch. It started off slow but we were finally able to cuddle while watching a movie. I held her while she leaned back onto me. For that alone, the night was a success. The movie made us gasp at times, at other times we got very quiet. Viv knew what she was doing.

By the end of it we were making out and lost interest in whether the two women would ultimately be together. It was only 10:30 p.m. – too early to watch Dick Clark and too early to "go to bed." I asked her if she wanted a drink. I did not drink but it was New Year's Eve and I had Cokes and knew my dad wouldn't miss a little rum. She agreed. I only mixed in a little rum, but it was enough to make us a feel a little grown up. She asked me if I wanted to see what was in her bag. I did. She had lingerie, a scented candle, and massage oil. I laughed and asked where she got it. She said she stole it from her Mom's bed table. We decided to forget about Dick Clark and who cares what time we went to bed. We went upstairs to my room.

She went into the bathroom with her bag. I lit the candle – my room didn't even look like my room in that light. I popped in my mix tape and hoped it didn't seem too cheesy. The rum and Coke had given me a little more courage. But mostly, I was just excited to be alone with her. To be able to kiss and touch without being worried that someone would catch us. I couldn't decide what to do about my clothes. I knew she was changing but I didn't have anything sexy. I took off my pants and just left my t-shirt and purple paisley panties on. I took my bra off. That was pretty sexy, right? I sat on my bed and waited. Prince sang "Adore." She came out.

I had seen women in lingerie before – Macy's ads, Victoria's Secret—heck, I had my own camisole with a fancy bra and panty set that I got for Christmas. But I had never seen another woman, in real life, in my room, with lingerie on. I really hadn't even imagined or dreamed of it. My fantasies were much more tame and involved lots of romantic kissing and handholding, beach walking towards sunsets. But when she stepped out in a low cut rose satin slip with matching bikini panties, any doubt I had at all about whether I was a lesbian or if this was a phase, or if I was just in love with Candace and maybe it would not be the same with other girls—that doubt vanished. My mix tape was playing, the candle was lit, and she walked out and looked at me. I wanted her. Oh, I loved her and I was nervous, but I wanted her.

I walked over to her and held her, softly exploring the texture of the slip and the feel of her bare shoulders. We kissed and it quickly became passionate tongue kissing. I had never felt so excited and so powerful. I could feel the goose bumps on her arms. I kissed her neck, her shoulders; I turned her around and kissed her back. I licked a line up her neck and heard her moan. I reached around and cupped her breasts. I could feel her nipples hard under the slip. We edged over to the bed and I took that slip off. She turned and pulled my t-shirt off over my head. We stood there in our panties, breasts touching. She reached around to grab my behind, I bit her gently on the neck and we giggled.

This was new for both of us, but we loved each other and it felt so right. We forgot about the massage oil and lay down together, luxuriating in the time we had, in the comfort of a bed and in the feel of each other's body. That night we tried everything we had heard about, everything we had read about and some stuff we just made up as we went along. It was a marvel, it was joyous, it was astonishing, and it was satisfying several times over. By about four in the morning, we were exhausted, but we had the presence of mind to change our clothes, open the window a crack and hide our contraband.

As we lay down to sleep, she whispered to me, "Happy New Year's, Dee. I love you so much. I'm so glad you were my first." She kissed me.

"Happy New Years, Candace, I love you more, now and forever," I replied and we fell into a deep, happy sleep.

The plane "dinged." Time to put on our seat belts and land, my least favorite part of flying. Viv and I rent a car and drive to the Westin Peachtree Plaza in downtown Atlanta. It was a lovely little suite, but more than I thought we needed.

"Why the suite?" I ask.

"Well, if you don't get lucky with Candace, I thought we could go to whatever the girls' club is down here and you know, hang out."

"Aren't you in a relationship? A monogamous relationship, Vivian Mellifluous Dupree?"

"Yes, but isn't this a ROADTRIP!!!" she laughs. "Seriously, I probably won't do anything, but can't a girl fantasize? I've been with Morgan over three years, which for me, you know, in dog years is like 21 years!!! Plus, I've been in a little apartment in Brooklyn, a fourth floor walk-up; I wanted to spread out a little. Let's go get some dinner. Then we can make it to the bar by 9 or 9:30."

"We're going tonight? I thought we would rest and maybe we would go tomorrow."

"Why wait? We flew down here to find the girl. Let's find the girl. Let's eat first but then let's find the girl! OK, I need to change into something decent." She looks me up and down and smirks. "You should change, too."

Over an excellent seafood dinner at a local restaurant, Viv catches me up on her new career in marketing for a local TV station. It was an unusual step for her, as she always wanted to be in the spotlight, not working for the spotlight. I have the distinct feeling that we are both somewhat dissatisfied about our lives. She calls Morgan from the restaurant and while she keeps it light and breezy, I can tell it was forced. I look at her when she hangs up.

"OK, we're having some problems," she says.

"What's the problem?" I ask while hailing the waiter for another *Pinot Grigio*.

"It's so typical, it's laughable. She wants kids, I don't. She wants to buy a house, I don't. I want to move to California, she doesn't. We love each other, really love each other, we live well together, have fun together, have great sex, you know, the whole nine. Now we've just reached a point in our lives where we both want to make a change, but it's not the same change. She wants to set down roots, and start a family life. I want to live in Cali, where it's warm, where there are more opportunities, and more fun." Viv looks resigned.

"Oh, well, now that would be a problem. How do you think you'll resolve it?" I ask.

"My guess is that we won't. We'll hem and haw for another six months or so, but in the end I'll have to leave and I'll be on my own again," she says.

"So, you'll just abandon the love you have? Don't you think that's a little callous? We aren't promised to find someone who'll love us, but now that you have, can you really walk away like that?" I ask, feeling somewhat irritated.

"Unfortunately, yes. If I buy a house and have kids and don't really want them, eventually I'll be resentful and feel trapped. If she moves with me and leaves everything she loves including the idea of a baby, she'll get resentful and hate me for it. It's a deal-breaker and this deal is broken," she says.

"That's so sad," I say.

"Yup, which is why getting away this weekend is good for me. It's hard living with this big ass elephant in the room," she laughs. "Hey, let's get going. At least one of us should find happiness, right?"

We pay up, tip well and head off to the Diamond Bar in Piedmont Park.

The outside of the bar looked pretty seedy. It was sandwiched between a laundromat and a check-cashing place, the paint old and peeling, and the neon sign was missing the "i" and the "B". We walked in though, and were pleasantly surprised. The bar was hip, clean, and busy. Most tables were occupied with couples having a late meal, the pool table in the corner was hosting a friendly game between twin brothers, and there was a jukebox playing R&B hits.

The bar itself was a huge circle in the middle of the room, and it was packed with young and old alike enjoying the charismatic bartenders – a sexy older woman with prodigious cleavage and a tall, muscular young man with a loud, booming laugh, also with a low-cut shirt. We sit on the woman's side.

"Two Jack and Cokes, please," I order.

"Ahhh, two serious women, I like that," she replies and winks at me. I catch a flash of her gold tooth in the back. Between that, her cleavage, and the Chaka Khan playing, I was starting to like this bar. She came back with nice, strong drinks in highball glasses and pushed a bowl of bar nuts our way. Viv puts a twenty-dollar bill on the table and leans forward.

"I'm Vivian and this is my friend, Dee. We were wondering if the owner, Kevin Wright is here tonight," she says. The bartender looks at us searchingly, and then smiles.

"Naw, something tells me you two are not here for child support payments. Kevin should be in 'round 11:00, he likes to be here to close the bar," she replies. She winks at me again and moves on down the bar where another customer is looking anxiously her way. I admit it; I checked out her ass. I couldn't help it! Viv catches me and laughs.

"Maybe you're just horny. Did we fly all the way down here to Atlanta because you're horny?" Viv smirks.

"Nooooo," I say. "Actually, after I broke up with Pepper, I did something I've never done before."

"Do tell, Miss Dee, I could use a good story to go with this drink," she says, taking a sip.

"Well, after an uptight little soiree I was invited by my 'perfect couple' patient to The 12th Street Bar...." I told Viv the whole story with all the lurid details, and I didn't even have to embellish much to impress her.

"Well! Now, that has made my day! I see you are a completely liberated woman. Still no U-Hauls for you, Miss Thing!" she exclaims clinking my glass. I motion for the bartender to hit us again, but Viv's comment strikes a little nerve.

"You know, I can be serious with one woman, if it's the right woman," I say.

"Sure, sure, I know, that's why we're here. To find the right woman and see if the shoe still fits," she laughs. "OK, we should figure out how to come off to this Kevin guy. We don't want to seem too much like stalkers."

"Right," I say. "We could say that we also went to Spelman and are looking for her."

"No," says Viv, "we don't know enough details to pull that off. Maybe we could say we just happened to be down here from Philly and decided to look her up."

"Yeah, but how do we explain that we know to look here? We are stalking her, aren't we?" I ask.

"Yup, we are, but it's in the name of love.... OK, let's just stay as close to the truth as possible. We were all close friends in high school; we're taking a get away weekend down here and decided to look for our long-lost friend. And I can tell him about Brian, etc. That should suffice, don't ya think?"

"OK, I'll try not to look desperate," I say.

"Oh, you never look desperate, sis. Maybe it's your medical training, but you always look cool as a cucumber. I like your hair this way, by the way, makes you look six inches taller...."

We while away the next hour chatting with the other bar patrons and the bartender. We order some sweet potato fries and chicken wings. By 11:15, I start to get anxious.

"He's not coming tonight, is he?" I ask.

"It's Friday night, it's his bar, so he'll be here. What else do we have to do anyway?" Viv replies. The crowd is starting to get a little noisier, a little rowdier, and a little rougher around the edges. I do not want to be here around two or three, whenever they close. Then we see a big, husky, but good-looking guy around our age come through one of the Employee Only doors. He is light-skinned with a baldie and a sandy goatee – big enough to be imposing, but not threatening.

He comes back behind the bar and greets the bartenders. He then begins serving drinks, making his way around the bar, saying "hello" to the regulars, flirting with the ladies, joking with the guys. He seems like a nice guy. I thought I would be jealous but I'm not, I just want to know where she is. He makes his way around to our section of the bar while we try to be casual and make small talk. The bartender comes over and introduces us to him.

"Kevin, these are the ladies who were looking to talk to you. Vivian and Dee," she says, all business. I am stunned that she remembered our names and when did she give him warning?

We say hello all around and Viv compliments him on the bar.

"So," Kevin says, "what can I do for you fine ladies this evening?"

Viv takes the lead. "Well, we were hoping you could help us find an old friend of ours."

"And who would that be?" he asks.

"We went to high school with a girl who came down here for college. She went to Spelman. My cousin, Brian Jeffries, said you knew her, Candace Wheeler?" she asks.

His tone changes from charming and in charge to bitter and defensive.

"Candace!" he spits out. "Yeah, I knew her. I was going to marry her." He turns away and grabs a bottle of Ketel One off the shelf. The bartender closes her eyes and shakes her head. I have a feeling that this is not going to end well. Kevin pours himself a shot and throws it back.

"So you knew Candace? From high school? I'm curious, was she a lying bitch then too?" he asks quietly. Uh-oh.

"Um, well, no, not to my knowledge. We were good friends, but we all lost touch after we graduated, so we thought...." I stammer. I do not want to get this big man upset.

"Good friends, huh, what did you say your names are?" he asks.

"I'm Vivian, she's Dee or Deirdre," says Viv hesitantly. She moves protectively towards me. Hell hath no fury like a man scorned.

"Dee, Vivian.... I don't remember her ever talking about a Vivian or Deirdre and we were together for almost four years. Maybe it's another Candace Wheeler?" he asks. He might be scorned, but he sounds genuinely concerned that we have the wrong woman. Oh, he was a nice guy at heart, but she must have hurt him deeply. He reaches into his back pocket and pulls out his wallet. He hands over a picture.

"Is this the woman you're looking for? This is my Candy," he says.

I take the picture and my heart skips a beat. It's a standard studio photo with a white background. She's wearing a white shirt and jeans. It's Candace. She looks the same as she did, still beautiful, maybe a little wiser, maybe a little more mature and her hair is longer. But it's my Candace. A lump rises in my throat. I swallow it and try to play it cool.

"Yeah, that's Candace, right Viv?" I say handing off the picture. I can't look anymore.

"Yeah, she looks the same," she says happily. "So, it seems like this may be a sore subject, but do you know how we could get in touch with her?"

Kevin takes his photo back, puts it neatly back into his wallet and shoves the whole thing into his back pocket. Then he pours another shot of Ketel One.

"Would you like a shot?' he asks.

"No, we're drinking Jack and Coke. I don't think the two would mix," I say.

"Right—Gloria, can you get two Jack and Cokes for these nice ladies, on the house." Then he turns to us, does his shot and leans on the bar. "I don't think I can help you, but since you're here, maybe you two can help me. If you know Candy like you say you do, and I'm not sure that you do seeing as she never mentioned your names, but maybe you know something I don't know."

We settle into our drinks and lean in.

"Candy and I met during our freshman year; I was at Morehouse, and she was at Spelman. It was a typical college relationship with some small problems, but mostly we were both serious students who had plans and no time for petty drama. We fit well together and she was the best thing about my time in college. We had plans to marry after graduation. I had not proposed, but we both knew I would when I had a job and a ring. I never cheated on her although I had opportunities and I could be stupid, but I don't think she ever cheated on me. Anyway, our first year out of college, she lived with some friends and I moved back home to save money, and then came New Year's Eve. For some reason, she was always emotional on New Year's Eve—I think it had something to do with her family...."

No Kevin, it wasn't her family. Absurdly, I feel a sense of pride. She was still thinking about me, even through college. I have a small but flickering hope.

He continues, "...but this last one, my family had a party here at the bar. We came dressed up and looking good. We danced, did some drinking and I thought we were having a good time until midnight came and she started to cry. I hugged her and asked what was wrong. She said 'Nothing and everything. I'm sorry.' Then she kissed me and ran out the door. I tried to follow her but got caught in an altercation. I called her that night, the next day, all day. I gave her some time and called a couple of days later and her friends said she had moved out. She didn't leave any information, she just left."

He pours and drinks another shot. He sighs and looks around. I feel sorry for him.

Kevin looks us in the eyes and says, "I'm not too proud a man to say that I loved her with all my heart, and that when she left me, she broke me. But what hurt the most is that she left without telling me why. I have no idea what I did or did not do. She just up and left. I haven't talked to her since." He leans back on the bar. "Now, do you know why she might have done that, old friends of Candace?" he asks. "Did she leave another brother back in Philly, or something?"

"No," I say, "as far as I know, she didn't leave anybody behind."

"I don't know why she would have done something like that," says Viv. "She always seemed very caring and honest to me. It doesn't seem like her to just leave like that."

Kevin sighs. "Yeah, I know." He pours another shot.

"Hey Kevin," I say. "What did she end up majoring in? What did she want to be, if you don't mind me asking?"

"I don't mind. For a while she talked about nursing and working overseas for non-profits but we all talked her out of that, of course. She graduated with a degree in education. She decided to be a teacher."

"Oh, that's interesting, thanks," I say, meaning it.

"Yeah, thanks Kevin, sorry about Candace, really," says Viv.

"Sorry I couldn't be of more help. If you do find her, tell her…tell her…." He shakes his head. "Never mind … let me know if you ladies need anything else. I have some work to do in the back." He moves on down the bar and out through the Employees Only door. We watch him go, finish our drinks, pay and leave. It's a heavy thing to feel all that heartbreak coming off a big ole nice guy like him.

❧

Later in our suite, as we lay in our beds thinking our own thoughts, I couldn't bear it any longer.

"You know Candace and I had our first sex on New Year's Eve, remember?" I ask.

"Yes, of course, I remember. It was a big fucking deal!" she laughs.

"Do you think it was me? Do you think she was thinking of me and that's why she left?" I ask.

"Of course," says Viv.

"Why didn't she come back home then—why didn't she come for me?" I wonder aloud.

"Maybe she wasn't ready to face you; maybe she needed to be alone. Think about it. She was with you through most of high school, then she was with Kevin through most of college, maybe she needed some space," Viv mumbles, then yawns.

"Yeah, but where did she go?" I ask quietly. Vivian snores.

The rest of the weekend Viv and I hang out just like old times, eating soul food, window shopping in a mall, and walking through Spelman's campus. I spend a lot of time thinking about Candace and imagining what her life was like down here. When I first found out about her long-term relationship with Kevin, I was jealous thinking that she had found happiness with someone else, a man no less. After his story of her abrupt departure, I worry that she's unhappy and has been unhappy all along. I wonder if she's living a miserable, closeted existence. I wonder if she regrets our relationship.

Saturday night, we find the gay girls club and go. Viv finds a few cute women to dance with, but I spend most of the night searching faces for Candace, wondering if she secretly knew any of these women or if she stayed away from women altogether. By the end of the night, I am exhausted and tired and no closer to Candace. In fact, I feel farther away.

Sunday evening, Viv and I are saying goodbye in the Newark Airport parking lot. Morgan came to pick her up. I look in the car and wave to her. I look back at Viv.

"Good luck," I say.

"You too," she says. We hug goodbye and she drives off with her doomed relationship. I find my car and drive back to Philly to my empty apartment.

❦ CHAPTER THIRTEEN ❦

By the middle of the week, I have finally caught up with my patients, my paperwork, and my appointments. I meet my sister downtown at Crimson Moon for coffee and to catch her up.

"So," she drawls, "Did you find Candace down there in Hotlanta?"

"No, but we did find her trail of heartbreak," I countered and then held my silence as I sipped my iced coffee with a shot of banana.

"OK, I'll bite. What are you talking about?" she asks. So I tell her the whole story. I leave out the part about Viv's doomed relationship. It was too personal. And Janine never liked Vivian, so I don't want her to gloat.

"So she's a teacher? Well, she could be doing that anywhere…. I hate to help you, but have you tried tracking her down through Facebook?" she asks hesitantly.

"Of course, but nothing comes up with her name, and she's not friends with any of our friends from school. I even 'inboxed' some people who I thought might know, but nobody has seen her or knows where she is. It's crazy!" I exclaim.

"Hmmm…. She's a teacher…. Maybe she was inspired to be one because of one of her teachers. Have you reached out to any of them? Maybe she got in touch with them for some career advice or something."

My heart starts racing. Janine is right. I had not thought about teachers. I can barely get through my coffee. I just want to get home to my laptop. Janine, however, will not be denied her evening out and she regales me with tales of her graduate courses, goofy classmates, and the horrors of living back home with our parents.

Finally back at home, I get on Facebook and search for my high school teachers' names. Not a few of them are on Facebook, but I absolutely cannot 'friend' all of them. It's just too weird. I try to remember which teachers Candace really liked and it hit me – Ms. Brown of course. Now what was her first name??? After looking that up (and it took a while since she no longer teaches at Girls' High) I copy it into the search bar, 'Susan Brown.' Ms Brown's face pops up third in the list. I click her page hoping she's lax on the privacy settings, but no, her page is on lockdown. I send the friend request and hope to God she remembers who I am and that she 'friends' former students. I cross my fingers.

On Saturday morning, I get another invite from Leslie to a ladies tea. I don't do tea dances, so I decline, but get the hint to call their friend. I spend the morning relaxing and checking Facebook every few minutes. I decide to call Noema that afternoon.

It is a beautiful day, and I think for sure that everyone and their mother will be out enjoying the sunshine. Wrong. It's 3 p.m. and Noema is home. I'm a little suspicious right off the bat, but I brush it off. Even though I spent the morning doing nothing, and I am at home at 3 p.m. still doing nothing, should I be ostracized for it?

"Hi. This is Dee, Laurie and Leslie's midwife. We met a couple of weeks ago," I say rather stiffly.

"Yes, hi, Dee. I'm glad you called. I was just thinking about you," she replies.

"Oh, yeah? What were you thinking?" I ask.

"I was thinking about calling you because you were really taking way too long!" she jokes. Her voice has that cute girl sound to it. Every other word has a slight crack to it making her sound unsure and yet amused at the same time. I find it charming and can't stop smiling. Uh oh.

"Ah, well, you know, it's been busy at the office, dear. Babies being born and all that jazz," I say affecting a high society accent.

"I hope that's not always going to be your excuse, darling, because that will only get you so far, Miss Midwife. You won't leave me sitting around with my meatloaf drying out."

I laugh. "You are very funny for an artist, Miss Noema. I thought artists were serious types with lots of serious things to express."

"Oh, I can bring the serious shit, but I save that for serious art lovers and critics. You don't strike me as either." I laugh. What the hell! She seems like she could be fun, and there is the business of that tattoo.

"Well, you're right about that. I'm just a simple girl, with simple tastes…. Hey, what are you doing this week? Would you like to go out and get some dinner, Miss Artist? I know a great place with some very interesting decor," I say.

"You are out of luck, Miss Midwife. I am all booked up this week, but maybe the following week? I might be able to squeeze you in on Tuesday, if that's OK with you?" she offers.

I'm a little disappointed, but I check my calendar and agree to that date.

"Great," she says, "I'll call you that Monday to confirm details, OK?" I can hear her smiling.

"OK," I say, trying to sound breezy about it. But I have this nagging feeling that I'm being lead on a little chase. I try to decide if I like it or not. "Bye, Noema."

"Bye, Dee. Enjoy the day!" And she hangs up. I stare at her card and feel a bit conflicted. She could be interesting.... But I'm looking for Candace. Right? I probably should not start anything while I'm still thinking about my first love, right? Isn't that why I let Pepper go? For space, for the chance to be truly in love ... again ... maybe.

I spend the rest of the day doing really boring tasks like paying bills, cleaning, and going through junk mail. Finally around 9 p.m. I feel caught up and decide I want to have some fun. But where? Not Marlene's, I might run into Pepper. Not Twelfth Street, I might run into Angel working her magic on some other hapless female. I just saw Bernie—Viv is back in Brooklyn, and my sister ... I just saw her too!

I decide to go to a movie. I check the times and there's an interesting foreign flick at the Ritz on Sixth Street. I head out, park in an overpriced lot, of course, and stroll into the theater ready to be swept away. I get a big bag of buttered popcorn and an orange soda and take a center seat. All around me are people on dates. Mostly older straight couples, but some younger artsy kids, two gay men holding hands, and a few single folks smattered throughout.

Then I hear it, the voice I just pegged as the cutest voice ever. It's laughing quietly, but I immediately recognize it. Suddenly the lights dim and the previews start. But I follow the sound of 'the voice' to the lower left side where I can see two women, heads close together, sharing a drink and looking very intimate. One has a baldie, the other has on a hat and on the back of her neck, the top of a familiar tattoo.

I try to ignore them for the rest of the movie, but I can't. I miss most of the film, glancing at them every few minutes. They don't kiss, but they seem very comfortable with each other. I leave just before the movie ends to avoid any awkwardness and go home wondering what's her deal? If she's dating someone, why is she going on a date with me? Why do I even care? I'm supposed to be looking for Candace anyway. I go home to bed, unsatisfied with my movie night, unsatisfied in general.

On Sunday, I decide to go for a run. It's so beautiful on Kelly Drive in the morning. The leaves are bright green, flowers are blooming, the air is warm and still spring fresh, and I am determined to do three miles. The Drive is full of new mothers walking their babies in strollers, veteran runners doing their usual five or 10 or 20 miles, and a slew of people who look like they are all trying to hurry up and get fit before summer is in full swing. I'm one of the latter. Huffing and puffing, I do my three miles and collapse on a bench. I check Facebook on my phone. Nothing.

After our glorious New Year's Eve, Candace and I were inseparable. Other friends and activities got slowly but surely edged into the fringes, and we became the center of each other's life. We were content to have everyone believe that we were just best friends and had formed that crazy tight sisterly bond that some girls do as teenagers. My parents were happy that I had a friend and her mom was happy that Candace was hanging with someone so academically ambitious. We got to have lots of sleepovers, of which we took full advantage, learning quickly how to make love as quietly as ninjas. We went to the movies, got jobs at the mall together, and I candy striped on the weekends while she spent her weekends singing in the church choir. We learned to drive that spring so that made things easier and we were both smart enough to keep up our grades. Occasionally, in school, I thought we got a few weird looks or I thought I heard somebody whispering. But we were very careful and went about our business, taking our PSATs and thinking about college.

The junior prom came and we had some decisions to make. We could skip it and risk suspicion or we could go with some boys we hardly knew and just try to have a good time. We debated it for a while, but in the end Candace's mom decided for us. She wanted Candace to go. She bought a dress and had a boy from church all lined up for her. His name was Chad Winslow. He was tall, dark, handsome, and gentle and I could tell he'd had a crush on Candace for a while. He was in the church choir with her. He sang bass. If she was going, I had to go. I found a boy through my Health Careers Club. He was the cousin of Jill, a future pediatrician or cardiologist depending on how it went. My date's name was Omar Jackson. He was OK looking, taller than me, which was all that really mattered in high school. My mom was worried about him being a Muslim, but I liked him because he was into music – he played the saxophone.

Candace and I had a long talk before the prom about rules. We both agreed that we had to seem like we were having a good time, but make sure they knew by the end of the night that we did not like them. Also, they could have one quick good night kiss at the door, but that was absolutely it. We decided to go separately to make it easier, but we decided to go to the same after-party at Shari's house, then IHOP, then home.

The prom itself was fine. My date was polite but funny and I thought I could probably be friends with him. My obnoxious fuchsia satin dress was itchy and the stockings impossible, but I had on comfortable shoes so that put me ahead of the majority of my limping classmates. We ate the bad food, sat at our table making small talk, and danced quite a few times. We both ignored the slow songs and enjoyed being sarcastic. Our prom picture would not have been horrible if I had kept my eyes open and if he wasn't smirking.

We talked a lot with Viv and her date, Stuart, some gorgeous gay boy she found at CAPA, the performing arts high school. I thought she was really testing her credibility, but everyone seemed to buy it. Maybe they were entranced with his green eyes and curly hair, but I thought it was funny. She fawned all over him and he played it cool. Actually it was quite an impressive performance and they produced a great prom picture out of it. I don't know how she knew him, but I never saw him again after that.

The problem that warm May night was Candace and her date. She looked elegant in her cobalt blue off-the-shoulder dress. He looked clean in his white suit and matching cobalt blue cummerbund and skinny tie. I would not have admitted it out loud, but they looked good together. I can't remember what their prom picture looked like as I tore it up immediately. Because they knew each other from church, they were already friendly and had a lot in common. He took the opportunity to really make a play for her. He would not keep his hands off of her, though they were sitting at a different table with other people from their church, and I could see him with his arm around her shoulder or a hand on her knee or whispering in her ear or touching her hair. I had to keep looking away and pretending I didn't see. Inside, I could feel a slow boil starting, so I turned to Omar for more jokes.

She told me later that he tried to feed her from his fork, had a flask with him that he kept trying to pour in her glass and three times, tried to get her to leave and go to the parking lot with him for a smoke. It's a good thing I didn't know that then. When they danced, he kept sliding his hand lower and trying to talk all in her ear. I could not tell what she thought of his attention. Sometimes she would smile and it seemed like she was flirting back—sometimes she seemed to be annoyed. I tried not to watch but as the evening went on, I was fed up with the whole scenario.

I was finally able to talk to her in the ladies' room by the sinks.

"Candace, what is going on with your date?" I asked in a whisper.

"What do you mean?" she whispered back.

"Why is he all over you? Why are you letting him be all over you like that?" I demanded. The jealousy monster I'd been suppressing all night was threatening to break out of the little cage I'd made for it.

"I know, he's very touchy-feely, but he's always like that. I don't take it personal; I just keep telling him that I'm not interested. Don't worry. I got it under control," she said.

"What do you mean 'He's always like that'? At church? Candace, seriously, tell him to keep his dirty hands off of you. I can't…. What are you smiling at? I'm mad," I angrily whispered to her.

"I can see that. So this is what you look like when you're jealous? Interesting, very interesting," she said. She looked quickly around; we were alone, and she quickly kissed me on the lips. "Dee, you have nothing to worry about. He's just a boy, a stupid boy. I can handle him. Now, how's your date?"

"He's fine," I mumbled, "nice actually, but that doesn't mean I would let him feel me up."

"I'm not letting him feel me up, I'm playing the game we have to play to be together," she said.

Two girls came in giggling and hiking up their pantyhose. Our conversation over, we re-applied our lipstick and went back into the fray.

The prom finally ended, and couple by couple we drifted to Shari's house. As expected, it became a drinking, grinding, making out party with a few indiscreet and tacky souls having some kind of sex in the corners. Omar and I arrived fairly early. We ate pretzels and talked about how lame high school was. I wanted to get out of there and I could tell Omar did too. He kept talking about real food like pancakes and sausage patties. He asked if I wanted to leave but I said no. Maybe he thought I wanted to 'get busy' because then he leaned in and tried to stroke my arm. My look sent him back to his seat looking relieved. I was not leaving until I had Candace with me. She and Chad finally arrived looking winded. She grabbed my arm and whisked me upstairs for "girl talk." We found an empty room. It looked and smelled like a baby's room.

"Ugh, I have got to get rid of him," she complained.

"Oh, is loverboy finally getting on your nerves?" I sneered. "What were you doing? What took you so long?"

"He insisted we take a drive. He asked me to be his girlfriend! Yuck!" she said. "I told him absolutely not. Now he's trying to play this hurt victim thing and convince me that the least I could do for him would be to have sex with him, you know, to help him get over his sadness."

I laughed. "Is he for real? What an asshole! OK, let's think of a way to get rid of him," I said.

"In a minute," she said, "there's something I've been wanting to do all night." And she pulled me close to her and kissed me. We made out passionately and thoroughly for a good 15 minutes in that powder blue room until we heard Omar's voice coming up the stairs. We pulled down our dresses, straightened up my pantyhose and fixed her bra. We both pulled out our lipsticks as the door opened to Omar standing there looking bored, bewildered and bereft all at the same time.

"Um, Candace? Your date is getting drunk; you might want to see about him. Dee? I'm hungry! Can we go?" Omar asked.

"Absolutely!" I said. "Candace would you like to go to IHOP with us?"

"Yes," she replied and smiled at me. I loved her so much at that moment. We left Chad at the party pseudo-sobbing to some poor sucker and went and had some pancakes with whipped cream.

❧ CHAPTER FOURTEEN ❧

Monday morning's early meeting is not about me but about business falling off. I've been so preoccupied I didn't really notice, but I realize I do seem to have more free time than I used to. We come up with ways of advertising and decide to do more community outreach. I'm thrilled. I need something distracting to put my energy into and this is perfect. I volunteer to help with everything. After the meeting, Meadow comes up to me and asks about my trip.

"I caught up with an old high school friend, and it was fun," I say.

She looks at me quizzically. "Then why do you look so sad?"

"I'm not, just tired I guess. I'm sorry I've been so distracted lately. We were looking for another old friend of ours, but we didn't find her. But I'm back now. Let's go find us some pregnant women, OK?" She lets me change the subject.

"OK, let's go!" We link arms and head back to our offices.

Unfortunately, my very first appointment is with Laurie and Leslie. Has it been a month already??? I put on some Erykah Badu – "Green Eyes" comes on, my eyes start to tear up at the first note, I skip past it. "Bag Lady," uh oh, skip, "Window Seat," OK, forget it. I put on some jazz instead. I get out my patient files, light a peach-scented candle, and try to prepare for Leslie's questioning. Maybe I can quick call Noema before they get here. I find her info and hit "call". She picks up on the third ring.

"Hello?" She sounds rushed.

"Hi, Noema. It's Dee. I'm sorry, but I can't make it tomorrow. I'm really swamped at work this week."

"OK," she says, "How about Friday night? Let's go out and have some fun."

"Friday night is great, and yeah, I could use some fun. I'll pick you up at 7 p.m.," I reply. Just as I hang up, my office phone buzzes; Laurie and Leslie are here for their six-month appointment. 'Ha!' I think, 'take that, Leslie!'

❧

The week goes by quickly. It's mostly consumed with work. I stay late every day working on outreach and catching up with my patients. I decide to start running on a regular basis so I get up early to get a mile in before work everyday. It's working. I'm early up jogging to an audio book, and then work all day, late to bed watching bad TV. There's hardly any time at all to think about Candace. Friday comes and I'm looking forward to this date with Noema. It will be a great distraction; I just hope she doesn't ask too many questions.

I make sure I'm outside her place before 7 p.m. She lives in Bella Vista, which is a cool neighborhood, but the parking is a bitch on the weekends. I took a cab. She has the top two floors of a converted row house. She buzzes me in and I walk up three flights. The door is open and she's waiting for me. I'm glad I've been running this week. I'm only panting a little, but my thighs are burning some. She invites me in. Her place is gorgeous. Gleaming hardwood floors, white walls filled with artwork, built-in shelves filled with books, and a spotless kitchen filled with shiny stainless steel appliances. I feel like I walked onto a movie set. I look at her and can tell she's been cleaning all day…for me.

"This is beautiful, Noema," I say, starting to walk around and look at the artwork. "Is all this yours?"

"No, actually only a couple are mine. I like to trade with my friends sometimes. Keeps us honest—keeps us inspired," she replies. "This is mine," she says. She points to a huge canvas covered in a vibrant swoosh of orange, red, and yellow. There is a thin line wavering through the center and then zooming off the frame and onto the wall. I love its energy. Underneath there is a little placard that reads, "orgasm series 2/14." I raise my eyebrows at her. She blushes and moves away to give me the rest of the mini-tour.

She has made a 7:30 p.m. reservation at a Moroccan restaurant within walking distance, so we rush out and take a quick walk to South Sixth Street. It's elaborately decorated, dimly lit and tinkling with Middle Eastern music. Thick rugs on the floor serve as our seats, the appetizer is a hookah passed around tasting of fresh apples and ginger. She is good company – funny, talkative, accommodating.

Our main course comes with a belly dancer that she seems to know. She gives me a little extra attention and I am not sure what to do. Dollar bills would probably be inappropriate. They both smile and tease me because I can't keep my eyes off her super low skirt and softly rounded belly. The dancer pulls Noema up to dance with her and she does, tucking up her shirt and revealing her dangling belly piercing. They perform a little routine for me and I am trying not to be charmed by this artist chick, but I kind of am. When the song is over, Noema takes her seat next to me and the dancer moves on to the next table. Noema sits down breathless and laughing; she gives me a quick kiss on the cheek and says "You're cute."

I smile back at her; she's not so bad herself. After dinner, we catch a cab up to Olde City. It's First Friday and all the art galleries are open. It's crazy crowded on this beautiful summer night, but we manage to squeeze into a few cool places. There's a trio playing some New Orleans jazz on the sidewalk and we find a spot to hang out and listen for a while. I look over at her and think, 'maybe?' I close my eyes, sigh, and look away.

"You OK?" she asks.

"Yeah, I'm great actually. I haven't been this relaxed in a while," I say truthfully.

"Relaxed? Oh, that's not good. Let's go dancing! I need to know if you can dance," she teases.

I shrug, "OK, where to? Where do you like to go?" I ask.

"Let's go to Shampoo," she says, hailing a taxi.

We get to the club around 11 p.m. and dance our asses off until 3 a.m. I haven't danced that long or that hard in a few years. I'm sweaty and my hair's a wreck, but I got my life and feel cleansed. God bless house music, all night long! Since we're close to my house, we cab it there to pick up my car so I can drive her home. I consider inviting her in, but it's late and I don't want her to sleep over. We drive back to her house content.

"Would you like to come in for a nightcap?" she offers.

"No, thanks. You have worn me out. But what are you doing next weekend?" I ask.

"Oh, I'll have to check my calendar, but I might be able to fit you in," she says.

"Thanks for a great night, really. I had a lot of fun," I say.

"Me too," she says. We lean in and share a quiet perfect first kiss. "Goodnight!" she says and hops out the car. I watch her walk in and try not to be excited. I think I like this woman. I drive back home, get in the house, and pass out all sweaty on top of my bed.

The next weekend's date goes just as well. We go to a Mexican restaurant on Chestnut Street, drink a pitcher of Margaritas then play pool and darts for the rest of the night at Buffalo Billiards. When I take her home, we make out in the foyer of her building but I don't go up. I'm a three-date girl. We make plans for the following weekend. We both are excited about it. I think she must be a three-date girl too.

❧

The week goes by fast. I check my Facebook several times a day, nothing from Ms. Brown. Maybe I'm not supposed to find Candace. Maybe I should just move on. I feel frustrated with myself. I call Viv.

"Hey Viv, how's it going?"

"Well," she says, "Now, we are seeing a couples counselor." It was her best friend's suggestion. "I think it's a waste of money, but it's something we'll do so we can say we really tried. Meanwhile, she caught me looking for work on the West Coast, and I caught her going through sperm donor profiles."

"Sorry," I say. There's not much more to say about that. "Yeah, well, I don't know about you, but think I'm tired of this whole love business."

"Yeah, I can dig it. Maybe I'll get a dog when I get to Cali." She laughs a sad little laugh and we get off the phone to deal with our own regrets.

That night, bored, I check my Facebook and notice that Ms. Brown had finally "friended" me! Ignoring her polite and warm message of greeting, I open Ms. Susan Brown's page and go straight to her "friends" list. It's over 500, which is a pretty good sign that she's accepting students as "friends." I scroll down to the C's, and then I go slow, savoring the search, not wanting to miss anything. I find Candace. The name says "C. Olivares," but the picture is of Candace. It's dark; she's sitting on a big rock. I click on her name.

Her page is also on lockdown but I can see where she lives, Albuquerque, New Mexico. Holding my breath, I google her new name and Albuquerque and she comes up in the local high school Web site as faculty. There is a picture. My heart leaps in my chest. She looks older and has a shorter, sensible haircut, but she's still beautiful. Her freckles are still where they were, her smile is still big and sincere. I found her. I can't believe it. I exhale. I can't stop smiling. She still exists. I am relieved. Now what? I feel conflicted. I call Viv.

"Hello?" she answers.

"Viv, girl, I hope this is a good time, because I have good news!!!" Unsure or not, I cannot stop smiling.

"What's up?" she exclaims.

"I found Candace! She's in New Mexico! Albuquerque, if you can believe it. She changed her last name, its Olivares," I tell her.

"Oh," Viv says, her voice dropping. "So she got married, then."

"Oh, yeah, I guess she did." My excitement waned some. "But at least I found her, right? I know where she works! But Viv, what should I do now? Facebook 'friend' her? That seems so lame. But I'm not sure I even want to do this anymore. I just started dating this other woman, Noema, who I think I really like. What would you do?" I ask.

"Honestly, I think I would go out there and see her. If you are wondering if she is still your true love, you'll know if you are alone together, in the same room. Online is too impersonal. It's just too easy to be dishonest or stretch the truth or sidestep it altogether. I say 'what the hell, go for it'!" She laughs, of course.

"Do you want to come?" I ask hopefully.

"Naw, Dee, this is all you, buddy, all you," she replies. She's right, of course.

"What should I do about Noema?"

"Didn't you just meet her, Dee? I wouldn't worry about it. You're just going to see an old friend, right?"

"Right," I reply, suspecting that it might not be that easy to convince Noema of that.

Luckily, I am wrong. I immediately call Noema and explain that I have just reconnected with my best friend from high school (leaving out the "girlfriend" part) and I am going to go see her and her husband in Albuquerque. So we put off our third date until I get back. Easy peasy.

CHAPTER FIFTEEN

The next week is a blur. I deliver two babies, complete another online workshop, and search for good deals for flights to Albuquerque. I meet with my co-workers to request more time off during the following week. They are none too pleased, and nobody is really buying my need for a spiritual retreat, except Meadow, of course. My chagrined and skeptical sister reminds me that since it is summer, Candace will not be in school and it might be harder to find her. She could be traveling or teaching somewhere else during the summer. More online searching gives me an idea what neighborhood she might live in, but I am really going on a wing and a prayer until the Sunday night before my flight.

I happen to check Ms. Brown's Facebook page one last time. She had posted something about Philly's humid weather, and as I watched, Candace made a comment. 'You should come out here for a visit, Ms. Brown. It's a beautiful, clear, sky blue day, and the cool breeze from the mountains is blowing the smell of my roses right through the kitchen window even as I write this.' I gasp. She was home right now! I was tempted, so tempted to 'friend' her to see if she would respond, but I resist by thinking about how great it will be to surprise her….and I'm scared shitless that she will ignore my request.

My heart beating faster, I shut my laptop, pack, get my things in order, and by Monday morning at 10:13 a.m., I am enjoying another lift-off. The flight to Albuquerque is fairly uneventful, but my thoughts are all over the place. I spend a lot of time trying to figure out what I am going to say, how I am going to explain myself, and what do I even want. The conversations with my sister come back to me. What am I willing to do? What do I expect her to do? I have way too many questions and no answers except the drumbeat of my heart and the surety that I am doing the right thing. I *had* to see her. I *had* to know that I was not romanticizing the whole relationship. I *had* to know that we did really and truly love each other and had meant something important and unalterable to each other. She was my first love, but the more I thought about it, she had been my only true love.

✣

The plane lands with a thud *bump bump bump*. I look out and all I see is beige and blue. This is definitely the Southwest. After an hour of waiting, I finally get my rental car and drive towards my McHotel in the Downtown area. Several times I almost have an accident. I cannot stop looking at the sky. It is incredibly big, infinitely bigger than the sky in Philly or DC or Atlanta. It is enormous and blue, a deep never ending blue. It is overwhelming. It is humbling. Maybe this will turn into a spiritual retreat after all. I feel naked, open to the universe under this vast sky. I think if I try even just a little bit, I can feel the weight of God on my shoulders.

I suddenly feel unsure of this journey. Am I up to this task? It started out as a lark, but now it feels so imperative. I hope I have not bitten off more than I can chew. But I'm here now. I'm going to try. I arrive at the hotel and even though it's a national chain, it still has that Southwest feel. I like it here so far. Something about being here is calming. I look out my window—they face the Sandia Mountains—beautiful.

But I'm not going that way. Candace, I think, is south of here in the Barelas. In my search, I learned that she teaches, goes to church, and is on the board of a recreation center in the Barelas. I pick up the complimentary White Pages and start to scan. It looks about the same as my internet search but it feels more legitimate to see it printed on paper. I run my finger down the list of names beginning with "O". There's something like 100 Olivares, three quarters of them living in the Barelas. There are no "Candaces," so I look at all the "C's." There are five. I write down the addresses and find them on my map. She could still be married and she might be listed under his name, but I have to start somewhere. But not today, it's almost 6:00 p.m. and I'm tired and hungry. I feel slightly lightheaded. I freshen up and go down stairs to find some good southwestern food to eat.

Tuesday morning, I cannot get over the mountains and the sky. How does anybody get any work done here, I wonder. I get a breakfast to go and with my nice strong *café au lait*, I head to the Barelas. It's a predominantly Hispanic neighborhood, old as the city, and filled with a mixture of buildings. There are some old adobe homes, some with Spanish-style architecture and others are a slightly more modern take on apartment living.

It's a busy morning and people are going about their daily lives. I am looking for C. Olivares #1. I find the first address and knock on the door. An older man named Carlos answers; he lives alone. I find C. Olivares #2 in an apartment building. A college student named Cari answers. I find C. Olivares # 3, but nobody answers the door. Someone is home and I can tell by the car in the driveway and the open windows with salsa music blaring, but nobody comes to the door. I go a-hunting C. Olivares #4. Connie answers the door. And while she is sweet and offers me a biscuit straight from the oven, she is not Candace and I move on. I have big hopes for C. Olivares #5, but they are dashed when three kids and a young woman with a baby on her hip named Consuela answers the door.

It's after 12:00 p.m., my stomach is growling, and I'm tired of meandering these old streets squinting at addresses and trying to parallel park this humongous SUV. But what the hell, I'm not too far. I circle back to C. Olivares #3 just in time to see a dark figure drive away in a red Jeep. I consider giving chase, but I'm not sure at all if that was even a woman. I'm tired, so I decide to do a stake out.

I drive to a local diner, Quirky Coffee, use the bathroom, buy a turkey and cheese sandwich, iced tea, and some chips. Then I go back to the house and wait across the street. I study the house. It's small but well kept. The front garden is full of blooming flowers and artsy and colorful outdoor garden sculptures. I wonder if this is what Candace's home looks like. I look for signs of children, but I don't see any toys. I consider checking the mailbox but decide I don't want to risk going to jail.

I wait. Various people walk by, older men going on a walk, teens on skateboards going wherever the local hang-out is, women with bags of groceries. It seems like a nice neighborhood. There is one figure, Kokopelli, who keeps showing up almost everywhere I look – in the airport, the restaurant, on street signs, even in the garden of this house I'm watching. I remember him as some kind of trickster deity, having something to do with fertility or babies. I decide I like his style. He seems frivolous with his dancing and flute playing, but he's everywhere, making babies and doing his thing, whatever that might be.

At about 3:30 p.m., I see the Jeep returning. It's coming towards me, but the sun in glinting off the windshield and I can't see inside. It parks in the driveway and I hold my breath. The driver's door opens and out steps a curvy, tall brown-skinned woman. She closes her door and opens the back door. She lifts her head up to the sun. It's Candace. I see her freckles, I see her smile, and I'm about to open my door when two kids pop out the Jeep with backpacks on, a boy, about nine or ten years old and a girl about seven. They look Hispanic with their straight black hair and light brown skin. They smile up at her and run up the porch. She laughs and runs after them trying to beat them to the door. They all go in and shut the door behind them.

I feel so stupid. What was I expecting? I hadn't really expected kids, cute kids who obviously loved her. Who was I to barge into her life? Her life looks just fine the way it is; she looks happy and healthy, her house is cute, her car is running and there are two kids who adore her. I sit in my car, paralyzed with indecision, stunned by my own stupidity. Why would I underestimate her ability to get her life together? An hour later, a man drives up in a Mustang and parks behind her car. Oh God! He must be her husband. I slump down in my seat. He gets out. He is tall, ruggedly handsome, and he looks athletic, dressed in shorts, a t-shirt, and a baseball cap. He has a whistle around his neck. I drive away.

I drive up into the mountains and park at a lookout. Up under the big sky, I search for answers. Why the hell did I come here? Why the hell did I fly out here? What the hell is wrong with me? I cry and cry my stupid little eyes out. She's fine. She's so obviously fine and happy. It's me with the problem. It's always been me with the problem. I watch the stars come out one by one. They grow brighter and brighter as the sky around them deepens—beautiful. It's getting colder, and my stomach starts growling. Numb, I drive back down the mountain, find my way to my hotel, and eat something in the bar there and drink red wine. I decide not to think. I watch some sports on ESPN and then go to my room. I can't call anyone, can't yet admit to being so ridiculous, so vain, so selfish, and just stupid. I sleep the good drowsy red wine sleep.

I wake up around 8:00 a.m. with a headache and loll in bed watching movies. I have a decision to make – leave without seeing her or go and see her anyway. Around noon, I make a list of pros and cons. Pros to seeing her – I see her and she sees me; maybe we'll become friends again or maybe those aren't really her kids and that's not really her husband. Maybe she is unhappy and will dump them and come away with me; maybe she'll take me on as a mistress or maybe she'll have become a bitch and smell funny and I suddenly won't care about her anymore or maybe I won't feel anything and I can move on with my life.

Cons to seeing her – maybe I'll realize how happy she is and get suicidal and kill myself … maybe she still hates me … maybe she'll pity me, or make fun of me, or think I'm crazy … maybe she'll realize that our high school relationship was so juvenile and just a silly stage or maybe she's gone religious and she'll curse me, or worse, pray for me; maybe she is miserable and she'll abandon her husband and kids; maybe she won't remember me, or if she does, maybe she'll belittle what we had; maybe she'll think I'm bitchy now or smell funny.

I spend all of Wednesday in bed thinking about the past. I'm still indecisive. Pathetic.

Thursday morning I get up and decide, "Fuck it." I came all this way. I have to see her if for nothing else than she knows that I still think about her and love her and want her to be well and happy wherever she is—whatever she is doing. Enough with the pity party! I bring babies into the world, damn it! I try to shake off my doubt. I get dressed in my 'cute butt' jeans and a beige button-down shirt. I'm trying to blend in a little. I venture onto the street and find a funky jewelry boutique and buy some turquoise earrings and a ring. My plane leaves tomorrow morning. I have one day to get this right. I eat a light breakfast at an outdoor café. I marvel at the sky and breathe deeply. I gather my courage.

I slowly drive back to Candace's house. The air is starting to heat up, and I'm starting to sweat. Did I put on deodorant? I hope I did, I know I did, right? I cannot remember and have a brief moment of panic. I cannot see her again for the first time in 15 years sweaty and smelly! I do it. I sniff…ocean fresh, whew!

I turn onto her street and see her cherry red Jeep in the driveway. The Mustang is not there. I park my rental and jump out. I walk to her house in a daze, barely feeling my feet on the ground. I can hear music as I get closer. I step up on the porch and see movement through a white lacy curtain. The window is open. I swallow hard, lift my hand, and press the doorbell. I can hear the ding-dong clearly. She's heard it too, the music lowers and I hear her walking across the floor. The door opens and she stands there, in a blue jogging suit, mouth open. We stare at each other.

I say, "Hi."

"Hi," she whispers, eyes wide. "What are you …?" She stops and looks around. "Come in, come in, OK?" She opens the door and steps back to let me in.

"I can't believe you are here," she says, shaking her head. "I'm sorry, I just can't … Dee, how did you get here? What are you doing here?" She is so shocked that I feel bad. Maybe I should have called or given her some kind of warning.

"Sit down," I say. I remember that I am a medical professional and the last thing I want is for her to faint or something. She sits on a big easy chair covered with watercolor flowers. I sit on the matching love seat.

"You look great!" I say, trying to break the ice. "I love this house, and your flowers out front are just beautiful." Silence.

"Candace, I'm so sorry to surprise you like this, but I've been thinking about you, about us and I guess I wanted to find you, to see you again, to talk to you again. It took a while to find you." I hesitate and try to figure out what she's feeling or thinking, but I can't. She's looking at the floor; she's fiddling with the rings on her fingers. I see a drop on one of her fingers, then another. I run to her and drop to my knees in front of her, grabbing her hands.

"Candace, please don't cry. I didn't come to upset you. Please don't be sad. I'm sorry. If you want me to go, I'll go. I just wanted to see you again," I say, desperately bowing before her, kissing her hand. Crying was never in any of my imagined scenarios.

"No, don't go. I don't want you to go. I thought I'd never see you again. I didn't want to see you again, but now that you're here…." She begins crying in earnest then and I reach up to hug her, to hold her.

"Candace, I …" I begin.

"Sshhhhh, Dee, you always talked too much." I hush and just hug her. I hadn't even thought about how much I missed something that simple. She smelled the same: clean, fresh, and just a little spicy like ginger. I felt her relax and release into my arms, I felt her exhale in my ear. It was truly like coming home again. I lean back and we look at each other. She smiles at me. I grin at her. I couldn't help it. I lean in to kiss her.

She leans back and says, "No, I can't."

"OK," I reply, "we won't." We let our arms down and separate. I stand up and take my seat back on the love seat. She reaches for a tissue and blows her nose.

"OK, Dee, how did you find me?" she asks. I tell her the whole story of my search for her, including Kevin and his heartbreak. She looks sad at that. When I got to the part about stalking her house two days ago, she jumps up.

"You were here, sitting outside my house, and didn't come to the door?" she exclaims.

"I saw you with two children, looking happy and busy, and then I saw your husband come home. I didn't want to disturb you when you were with your family, so I left," I explain.

"Oh, you saw them?" she asks.

"Yes. Candace, I came here…. I came here because my life, though parts of it are wonderful…. Hey, I did become a midwife, you know!"

"You did! That's great, Dee, that must be such a great job! You have to tell me about it," she exclaims.

"I will, but I wanted to say that my life is great in many ways but I have not found, um, I have not been, I have not found the right person yet. I have had plenty of girlfriends but I haven't been in love with any of them like … like I was with you. Once I realized that, I just couldn't stop thinking about you and wondering … wondering if you were that right person for me, you know, my true love." There, I said it! Whew! Her face is unreadable.

"But," I add, "I did not come here to interfere or mess up your life. I guess I just came to see … uh …."

"Hmm … lots of girlfriends? Have you just been with women then?" she asks, changing the subject.

"Yeah, just women. Well, one guy in college just to see, you know, but yeah, all women," I reply. "What about you?"

"Me?" She sighs. "It's a long story, well, no, I guess it's not. After we broke up, my family watched me like a hawk. When I went down to Spelman I know there were girls there who reported back to their mothers, who reported back to my mother about what I was doing. Luckily, I met Kevin and he was nice and that worked just fine…until it didn't."

"That was some story he told us. It didn't sound like you to just up and leave somebody like that. It was cold." She is thoughtful.

"It was the only way I could think of at the time. I went down to Spelman to grow up and be independent, but I just changed hands. At home, I did what my mother told me, with Kevin, I did what he told me to do. By the time we were ready to graduate, I could see my life laid out in front of me, and it wasn't a bad life, but it wasn't of my making or my choosing, so I ran away," she says. "I'm sorry I hurt him though, he's a good guy. I just didn't have a good enough reason to leave, but I had to anyway, you know?" I did.

"I came out here to start a new life, away from all those expectations and pressures. I wanted to be somewhere else and this place is beautiful, don't you think?" she asks. I nod.

"So then you met your husband out here?" I ask, trying to sound polite.

"Yes, I met Ramon here. He's a math teacher and the baseball coach at my school. We got married five years ago," she said.

"Oh, are the children yours? They looked older...." I stop. I feel like I'm being rude.

"It's OK. Elena and Marcos are from Ramon's first wife. She is a drug addict though, so he has sole custody. I'm the only mother they know," she explains.

"Oh. Well, they look like great kids," I say, feeling like I have definitely intruded here and perhaps I should beat a quick retreat and save face.

"They are great. Smart, funny, and a lot of fun, actually." She lights up talking about them.

I'm happy for her, I truly am, but I am feeling a little jealous of her happy life. I'm a tragic, self-centered bastard. I know I am because in my heart of hearts I wanted her to be miserable so I could sweep in here, whisk her into my arms, and we could ride off into the sunset together. I'm pissed that's not going to happen.

"Listen," she says, "I'm a little overwhelmed by seeing you, and I have some stuff I really have to do before I pick up the kids from camp. When are you leaving?" she asks.

"My flight leaves tomorrow morning, 11:05 a.m.," I reply.

"Oh. Can we meet tonight for a late dinner or drinks or something?"

"Sure, but if you're busy with family, I understand, it's OK...." I try to give her an out.

"No, I really want to talk some more and I would love a night out, tonight, OK? What about 8:00 p.m.? I'll meet you at your hotel, OK?" she says.

"OK, I would love to," I say truthfully. We get up, exchange cell phone numbers, and hug goodbye. She walks me to the door and I leave reluctantly. She laughs and kisses me on the cheek. I know she watches me while I drive away. I put my sunglasses on and try to look cool.

I decide to spend the afternoon being a tourist. I wander through Old Town, I visit the Indian Pueblo Cultural Center, browse the shops in Nob Hill, and buy a cool birthing painting that would look perfect in my office. I buy a little wooden statuette of Kokopelli for the office too.

I get back to my hotel around 6:00 p.m., take a long shower and try to process the long day. Getting ready, I have to battle myself from falling into date mode. It's not a date; I do not have to shave my legs (but I do). It's not a date; I do not have to be fresh and trimmed (but I am). It's not a date; I do not have to have cleavage (but it's the only thing left clean!). It's not a date; forget the musky perfume you love (but I love it, so why not?). It's not a date, so calm the hell down (but I can't). At 7:55 p.m., I turn off the TV and take the elevator downstairs. It does nothing for my nerves. I walk into the lobby and I see she's already there. She's dressed like she's going on a date. She looks beautiful in her halter top and wrap skirt. I try not to swoon. We hug hello, she smells divine. I think I see her hands shake a little.

Earlier in the day, the concierge had given me the name of a hip but quiet restaurant nearby, and Candace and I walk there. It's a cool evening, but it feels good to walk together. We come to the restaurant and go inside, landing a table in the window. We sit and look at each other for a while. I can't believe that I am here, sitting across the table from Candace.

"Hi," I say. She laughs.

"Hi," she replies.

The waitress comes to take our drink order. I contemplate ordering something sophisticated or fancy, but

I need something for my nerves, so I order a Jack and Coke. Candace orders a white wine. I realize that I do not know this woman. Candace was once the center of my universe, but we've never even had drinks before, never talked as full-grown women.

"Hey," she says to the waitress. "This is my dear old friend from high school, would you take our picture?"

"Sure!" says the waitress. We pose, arms around shoulders, grinning from ear to ear. She takes a picture with both of our phones. I look at the picture; we look good together. We always did.

"So tell me about your life," she says and I do. Over grilled salmon and ginger rice, I tell her about college, nursing school, and being a midwife. I tell her about Viv, my sister, my townhouse, and Bernie's upcoming wedding. I gloss over the many relationships I've had and there've been a lot, so why get into it? I hit the highlights. Over roasted vegetable ravioli, she tells me about life and teaching in Albuquerque. She tells me about Elena and Marcos; she tells me about her estranged relationship with her mother and sisters. That makes me sad. I had a lot to do with that. I start to apologize, but she waves it away before it can get out of my mouth.

"I don't want to go back to that, OK? Let's just be happy to see each other again," she says.

"Ok," I say, "Tell me about Ramon then. I want to know about him."

"Ramon," she says, "well, how do I begin? Well, he's very athletic, loves to hike and run and play all kinds of sports. He's very good with our kids and the kids at school. He has a small family, but they've been in Albuquerque for 300 years. He is a genuinely nice guy...."

"Good!" I look at her. She's biting her lip. "What are you not telling me?"

"Actually, we're separated." She looks up at me. My heart skips a beat.

"Oh? Why?" I ask. I hold my breath.

"Wait," she says. She orders us another round. When her wine comes, she takes a big sip and sighs. "Ahhhhhh!" I look at her waiting, wondering. "OK," she begins. "This is embarrassing and I'm really very ashamed and I feel terrible."

I wait for it.

"I cheated on him, just once, just barely and he caught me." She looked chagrined but like she was suppressing a smile.

"If you feel so bad, why do you look like the cat that got the canary? I can almost see the yellow feathers in your mouth! What is it Candace?"

"I cheated on him with…the librarian," she says and busts out laughing.

"What!!! The librarian? Female librarian?" I ask. She nods, laughing so hard tears are coming out of her eyes. I laugh too, but I am confused. I had assumed she had not been with any other women.

"Candace! Get yourself together! What do you mean? I thought you were just totally with men now! I don't get it!" I say, somewhat exasperated. She takes a deep breath and calms herself down.

"Ooh, that was a good laugh. I needed that. It's been a rough few months. You are the only person who knows that I don't have anybody here or at home that I could tell that to. I'm so glad you are here." She reaches out and grabs my hand. "Truly, I have been living with so much guilt. I thought I would just crumble under the burden of it. Ramon is devastated. He also can't tell anybody what happened or he would be humiliated. Oh, I just messed everything up." She looks truly troubled now and she slides her hand back to her lap.

"OK, well why don't you just tell me everything so you can get it off your chest," I offer.

"Are you sure you want to hear all this? I'm pretty sure this is not what you came here for," she says.

"I came here for you, Candace. Tell me what happened." I sip my drink and listen.

"Well, first you should know that I have not been with another woman since you. Honestly, after I left Philly, I just wanted to put all of that behind me. My therapist and I were pretty sure that my relationship with you was a one time thing and that I was, you know, normal. I had a little crush at Spelman, but I never did anything about it, and then I met Kevin. When I first moved here, I had a yoga instructor who I thought was interesting, but again, I never did anything and I met Ramon shortly after that."

"Therapist? You had a therapist?" I exclaim.

"My mother made me go to a therapist for the rest of senior year and when I came home for visits – 'a check-up' she called it," she smirks. "Anyway, so I fell for Ramon, Elena, and Marcos, and we got married. The kids were all consuming; they were just two and four at the time, and I was still a new teacher. It was very busy those first few years. Anyway, like any married couple, Ramon and I had cooled off a bit, and during baseball season it's almost impossible to get his attention.

So in February, the school librarian, Lisa, asked me to help with re-organizing the library. We were friendly and I teach English so it was no big deal. Now I knew she was a lesbian, everybody did, and it was a big controversy for a while but then it died down. She's in her mid-thirties; she's also an artist and writer, a hippie type. We have lots of them here. She lives in a cool old adobe house not too far from here. Anyway, one day, we were moving books, in the aisles and we were talking about Octavia Butler's *Kindred* when I just kissed her."

"What? You just kissed her out of the blue? She could have smacked you!" I say.

"I know! No one was more stunned than me, except maybe her. I don't know where it came from, just all of a sudden we were so close together and she was nice and I guess she looked cute in her glasses?" Candace giggles. "It's not funny really, but it was completely unplanned and totally reckless."

"So then what happened?" I ask, waving us another round of drinks.

"Well, then she kissed me back and before you know it, we were making out hot and heavy. I was … overcome a bit. Then Ramon walked in. He was coming to get me for lunch. We pulled away as soon as we heard his voice, but he heard and he saw us. I was mortified. I tried to explain that it had never happened before, but he's convinced that we've been having an affair for years under his nose and no amount of me trying to explain has helped."

"Oh. So what about the librarian?" I wonder aloud.

"Oh, Lisa? We talked and we both regret it and whatever it was is over and done."

"It's just Ramon, huh?"

"Yeah, Ramon had just come out of that traumatic relationship with the kids' mother and now he feels betrayed by me. He moved out when the school year ended. He's staying with his brother. We're kind of sharing the kids until we figure it out," she says.

"Wow, Candace, that's some serious drama," I say.

"Yeah," she says. "I feel bad about Ramon. He's a good guy. I feel worse about the kids, they deserve better—they deserve a good mom." She bites her lip then looks at her watch.

"I should go. But it was so good to see you, Dee, *really* good." She drinks the rest of her wine and signals for the bill. I try to pay but she insists on paying. After all, I paid for the flight, hotel, and rental car. I didn't argue but worry when I see her stand up; she looks a little unsteady on her feet.

The night air sobers us up a bit. It's late and the streets are empty. When we get back to the hotel, she hesitates, and then asks to come up and use the restroom. In the elevator, she doesn't look at me. I wonder what she is thinking. In my room, we freshen up, then stand at the big picture window and look out at the mountains and the dark sky above. I turn on my little sound system to play Esperanza Spalding and dim the lights so we see less of our reflection and more of the stars. She shivers. I put my arm around her. She asks me to turn out the lights. I do. The stars are amazingly clear and bright; we step closer to the window to get a better look. She turns to me and kisses me. It is a kiss so full of love, of childhood memories, of affection, of regret, of longing and absence. It is our kiss as I remember it, but enriched with experience and knowledge. Wrapped together, we exchange breaths, each one reminding us of who we were together. She feels good, she feels right. I love her, still. And I know, I feel, that she loves me just the same.

Even so, when she pulls gently away and gathers her purse, I am not surprised. I knew she would go. I have my love and desire but she has her family. She was raised to be a good woman, a good wife and mother. I respect that about her. I hate that about her. At the door, she turns to look back at me and I see tears in her eyes but walks out without saying a word. I stand heartbroken looking at the hulking blackness of the mountain.

I leave New Mexico dwarfed by the unending sky, feeling empty, alone, and discontent.

💀 CHAPTER SIXTEEN 💀

Saturday morning, I wake up in my own bed and go through the motions of showering, dressing, eating, and laundry. I peek through my window—the trees are still green and lush but I feel cramped, like I can't breathe. The message light on my phone is blinking. I have four messages. First is my mom, who never calls my cell phone because she doesn't want to 'bother' me. Then Viv, who knew better than to call my cell phone while I was out there. Then Tracy Ann from work, leaving a reminder about an early Monday morning meeting – I hope it's not about me. And there is a message from Noema, checking on me.

I call Viv and tell her the whole story. She listens quietly.

"Viv, when I saw her, it was like I'd never been apart from her. I loved her, I knew her, I felt for her just the same as I did 15 years ago. I swear I could have swooped her up and married her right then," I say emphatically, only a little more dramatic for my second glass of red wine.

"Dee, you're crazy! What about that break-up? Did she forgive you for that?" exclaims Viv.

"I don't know, but it didn't matter. It's like I still knew her and she still knew me. I can't explain it. But she chose her family and I guess I can't be mad at her for that. I just wish I could have another chance with her...."

Viv sighs sympathetically. "Sorry it didn't work out, Dee. At least you know the truth now though, right?" I think she was almost as disappointed as I was. She too, was hoping for a little bit of 'love conquering all' business.

I decide to try and forget about Candace and just concentrate on Noema. She's beautiful, smart, and talented. I'd be a fool if I didn't give her my full attention. I spend Saturday cleaning and listening to reggae music. Scenes from my visit with Candace keep intruding – her laugh, her smell, her eyes when she smiled. But I am determined. I just keep pushing the thoughts out of my mind, shaking them off like a bad dream. I chant to myself, "I'm moving on. I'm moving on." I clean my entire house, I do all the laundry, I clear out all the old food and even some clothes. I recycle old junk mail, magazines, catalogues. I reorganize my books and my closet. I pull out some Iyanla Vanzant books and *O* magazines. By 5:00 p.m., I'm good and tired, and I actually take a nap. I can't remember the last time I've taken a nap. But when I wake up at 6:30 p.m., I feel great.

I call Noema and push back our dinner to 8:00 p.m. I need to get ready. I groom myself. New nail polish, freshly washed and coiled hair, new underwear. I decide to wear something slightly butch. I want to feel powerful and in charge. I put on my summer white cargo pants, a tissue-thin cotton brown button-down with a cowrie shell choker and matching drop cowrie shell earrings. I look at myself and wonder if Candace would have changed her mind if I had been dressed up and sexy. Quickly, I shake that thought off and restart my chant, "I'm moving on. I'm moving on." I add a big funky cowrie shell ring and wrist cuff and top it off with sandalwood oil and lip-gloss. I'm ready.

I pick Noema up and we head out to Café Curry, an Indian restaurant downtown. It's casual but clean and efficient, and the food is good. I have a Dark and Stormy to go with my curry chicken and cashews. She has a chardonnay to go with her Tandoori vegetables. I can't stop thinking about how good she looks in her white tank and leather vest with a mini skirt and thigh-high boots. We are usually easy with each other but tonight the conversation is a little stiff. She tells me a little about her new art projects for an opening she's having in December. I tell her about my day of cleansing.

"I feel like I'm ready to start a new chapter in my life. I'm ready to let go of some stuff I'd been holding on to and making room for new people, and maybe a new attitude," I say honestly. She holds her glass out to me and I tap it with mine.

"Here's to new people and new experiences!" she says.

"New journeys and new adventures," I add. We clink again and sip our drinks. When I close my eyes to savor my drink, Candace is there. I shake it off, open my eyes and look at Noema. By the time we get to dessert, I'm worried about this evening. It feels too soon, too planned and I know too well how too much expectation can ruin sex. I don't want to rush what should be a good thing. Instead of going home, I suggest we go to the Twelfth Street Bar. It's a risk, but I think we need to loosen up with some loud music and a gay crowd. We walk over there. It's a humid night in Philly, but that just means that the streets are jam-packed and we laugh all the way to the bar. We turn the corner to go into the alley and I stop her.

"I've been wanting to do this all night," I say. I hold her hands and kiss her. We are gentle at first but soon we heat up. Several people walk by and stare. I don't care, but she stops.

"Do you still want to go in?' I ask.

"Sure, we're already here but just one drink, then I want you to take me home." She gives me a look full of desire. I'm not sure I want to waste my time at this bar but she's pulling me along.

The music hits us full blast when we open the door, and we step inside and let our eyes and ears adjust. We pony up to the bar and she grabs the one free stool. I step in between her legs and kiss her neck. She orders our drinks.

"So," I ask. "I'm dying to know what your tattoo is."

"Oh, this old thing," she touches the back of her neck, "you'll find out in about an hour." She grabs my pants by the belt loops and pulls me closer.

"You smell awfully damn good tonight. I think I can just eat you up," she growls in my ear.

"Oh, you'll have your chance in about an hour," I say, laughing. Our drinks come and we scoop them up.

"Let's have at least one dance since we're here." I say.

"OK," she agrees.

We head upstairs and are in luck. They are playing classic house on the third floor. I whisper to the DJ, an old friend of mine, she nods and starts digging in her crates. A minute later Lil Louis' "French Kiss" starts to play; I blow a kiss to the DJ and turn to Noema. We dance and kiss and grind and kiss and finish our drinks, and by the time that 10-minute extended version is over, I'm ready to take her home. We dash out the bar, into my car, drive back to my house and barely get in my front door when I'm all over her. I thought I would be a little cooler, but she's looking so sexy. I drop to my knees and slide off her boots, kissing her up and down her legs. I kiss up her thighs until I reach her skirt then back down again and up the other leg. She finally grabs my head and pulls me up, I French kiss her long and hard while I slide my hand over her tank. I can feel a thin bra and her nipples harden under my touch. I squeeze them through her tank. She's pulling my shirt up out of my pants and unbuttoning the buttons. I slide my hand up under her skirt and in between her thighs. I can feel her wetness and I slide one finger under the side of her panties. We groan at the same time.

I murmur, "Welcome to my home. This is my living room…."

"Shut up," she says, "and fuck me please." I do as I'm told. We make our way into my bedroom, I quickly light a candle, turn on some music, and take off her clothes. She's beautiful, but I don't waste a lot of time looking, I dive right in and don't look back.

Some time after noon, I wake up and try to get moving, but I am stiff and tired. We fucked each other silly until we heard the birds start to sing and a delivery truck rumble down the street. Now, sex-stiff and funky, I roll over and look at her. She is beautiful and naked, in my bed, which looks like a tornado hit it, as does the rest of my bedroom. I look around. Massage oil, dildos – the big one and the small one, blindfold, harness, and clothes thrown everywhere. Oh, it was a good night. I haven't had a workout like that in a few years. My neck is stiff, my tongue sore. Whew!

I hobble over to the bathroom and try to get it together. After a long shower, I come out and Noema is still asleep but now she's on her stomach. I go over to have a good look in the daylight. It's a tattoo of a dragon holding a human baby. It's very ornate and fanciful. The tail of the dragon is what curls up her neck. While the pose is gentle and kind, the dragon itself looks dangerous. The claws are super-long and its teeth are bared even though it's looking down at this tiny baby with love. It's quite disconcerting. I move away and start to clean up the room.

Noema wakes up an hour later. Coffee is on, the room is clean except for the bed, and I am dressed in shorts and a tank. She smiles up at me and croaks, "Coffee."

Despite our exhausting night, I still manage to go to my parent's house for Sunday dinner. I give a quick recap of my trip to Albuquerque, but I don't mention my disappointment. I don't have to. My sister does not say what's on her mind, but I see it written on her face anyway. I mention that I've started dating someone else and they all seem relieved. I go and watch baseball with my dad. We drink beer and munch pretzels. Good ole dad.

CHAPTER SEVENTEEN

When I get home from work on Wednesday, there is a letter from Candace. My heart skips a beat. I sit down to read it. My hands are shaking a little bit.

Dear Dee,

I hope this letter finds you well. I can't tell you how much your visit meant to me. I am so glad you found me and came to see me. I know that it was necessary at the time, but I regret losing you as a friend. You were the best friend I ever had and I will always value our relationship and that time in my life.

I'm writing just to give you an update. Ramon has agreed to move back in with me and he and I are going to commit ourselves to our marriage and move forward. We love our children and our family and our life. I thought you would want to know.

I wish you the best always. Thanks for reminding me of what is really important in life.

Love,
Candace

I crumple up the letter and bawl. There, that's it. I try not to care but my heart is aching. She knew I was waiting, she knows me well enough to know that in my heart I was waiting to see what Ramon would do. He took her back.

She's staying with him. That's it. Even though the sex was great with Noema, in my heart, I was waiting, hoping, not even admitting it to myself but now … I leave my food uneaten on the table and I give myself over to sobbing in my bed. It was not the first devastating letter Candace had written me.

The summer before our senior year passed much like the one before. Candace went down south for a month then on to Detroit with her dad. I did an internship program at Einstein Hospital and worked at a small bookstore on Germantown Avenue. I hung out with Vivian and her new girlfriend, Stacey. I took up jogging with my dad in Valley Green. I fantasized about college life all the time. I was applying to five schools and I was nervous. Candace and I shared three schools on our wish lists. We wanted to go to school together or at least near each other now that we could drive. My little sister Janine would be starting Girls' High in the fall. I tried to prepare her as best I could. When Candace was finally back in town in August, we went out to dinner at Dave and Buster's with her family. We had a great time. Candace drove me home that night. We parked on Kelly Drive and renewed our physical relationship in her mom's navy blue Oldsmobile. It was uncomfortable, but it had been a long seven weeks. I went home smiling.

Senior year started off pretty good. We were careful to do well academically for the first grade period; we both added a few extracurricular activities for our college applications so we were pretty busy. We were comfortable with each other and our relationship. But I began to have problems with all the secrecy. I was already somewhat of a big mouth, speaking up in classes and taking on leadership roles, and generally, I wore my opinions on my sleeve. I was starting to feel grown up and very confident in my belief that all people should be treated equally. But personally, I was beginning to feel oppressed and I was getting uncomfortable with it. I was in love, why should I hide it? I began to get reckless with my love for her. She tried to keep me in check and a few times, she playfully rejected my casual displays of affection. It stung nonetheless.

It took me a few weeks before I noticed the girl. Her name was Joan. She was new to the school. She had just moved here from Brooklyn. She lived near Candace and they ended up on the same bus to and from school. She was tomboyish with short hair and she was a little roundish. But she had dimples and a big laugh and she seemed to make friends easily. She made friends with Candace. One day I was standing near the front steps when I saw them get off the bus together. They were laughing, and she touched Candace on the shoulder and said goodbye as Candace turned to me. Over her shoulder, I saw Joan look at her butt! What the hell!! She looked up and saw me watching her. She smiled and gave a little wave and walked the other way whistling. I was floored and I was pissed.

"Candace!" I motioned for her to follow me further up the brick wall where there were fewer people around. "Who was that?"

"Who was what?" she replied.

"Who was that girl you just got off the bus with? The one you were laughing and giggling with?" I demanded.

She looked at me quizzically. "Oh, that's just Joan. She's new. She moved here from Brooklyn this summer.... Why are you looking so crazy?"

I whispered, "I caught her checking out your butt! That's what!" Candace didn't look too surprised. "Oh yeah?" she said.

"Yeah! And she knows I saw her and didn't seem to care at all!" I said.

Candace whispered, "Maybe she's a lesbian, whoooooo." She made scary witch hands at me and laughed. I was not at all amused.

"Maybe she likes you," I countered, "that ain't so funny to me."

"Oh, Dee! Stop being so dramatic! What if she does? So what. I'm with you and that's all that matters, right?" she cooed. The school bell buzz drowns out whatever I was going to say next. We turned and joined the mob going up the stairs. I was not reassured one bit. That girl was trouble. I could smell it.

For a few weeks, Candace tried to avoid the girl for my sake while I kept a wary eye out for her in the halls. When we did cross paths, she would nod and flash that dimple grin at me like we shared a secret. We did, but she was no co-conspirator with me. By the end of October, Candace was back on her regular bus and convinced me that she could be 'bus friends' with Joan without a problem. She told me I was acting immature. That hurt. Still, I sent Viv in to investigate. She came back with a report.

"OK, number one, it's too bad that you won't get to know her, she's quite funny and sarcastic, I think you would like her," Viv said. I glared at her.

"OK, number two, she is definitely gay. She told me right away. Her family knows and she doesn't care who knows; she's happy and fine with herself." I felt a pang of jealousy.

"OK, and number three, she did say that she had her eye on a girl here at school but she wouldn't say who. She knows that this is not a queer-friendly school and she doesn't want to start any trouble." I gasped. I knew it!

"Now Dee, it could be anybody. It might not be Candace at all. I think you should just chill out. She seems cool and I believe her when she says she doesn't want to start anything."

"Did you tell her about any of us?" I asked.

"No, I just told her about me. I told you, she seems cool. You should get to know her, you might like her," Viv said.

"Doubtful. Thanks, Viv," I said.

That night, I called Candace on the phone and told her what Viv learned.

"I want you to stay away from her. I can tell she likes you," I plead.

"Dee, you're being ridiculous, but maybe we should just tell her about us. I'll tell her we're a couple and then you won't have to worry," she said.

"I don't trust her. What if she uses that against one of us? What if she tells someone to get back at me?" I said. Candace thought that over for a minute.

"OK, well, what if I just tell her I'm seeing someone, at church, a boy. Then she'll know I'm taken. But seriously Dee, she's just a girl on the bus. I don't know why you are jealous. Don't you trust me?" she asked.

I did. I truly did. I knew she loved me and I loved her and we had a good thing. There was just something about that girl. Her smirk, her swagger, her cockiness, her loud boisterous Brooklyn laugh, and the stupid toothpick she sometimes chewed. She was under my skin. But Candace was right; I was acting like a jealous witch. I had to stop. I would continue to hate Joan; I just vowed to keep it to myself.

"OK, tell her the boyfriend thing just in case. I'll back off, OK? I just … I just didn't like another girl checking you out. I got jealous, I did. I admit it. I'm sorry, OK?" I confessed.

"OK, now just let me handle it. She's just a girl on my bus. But you, you are the love of my life, Dee. Don't forget that, OK?" she said.

"OK," I replied. But right before the Christmas break I did forget it. Big time.

Things had been fine. Candace told Joan the boyfriend thing and they still talked on the bus, but I didn't notice anymore eyeballing so I went back to my other worries — SAT's, college applications, my job at the bookstore, and my mom who was on my nerves. A few times I saw them laughing in the hallways and joking outside of school, but I vowed to trust Candace and I kept my suspicions to myself. I still refused to befriend her although Viv had. I was stubborn.

Then one day, right before the third period bell was going to ring, I was coming around the corner delivering some SAT prep work to the office when I saw them. They were coming out of the girls' bathroom together. Joan was tucking in her shirt and Candace was smoothing her hair down walking out first. Then she stopped and leaned back as if she was going to kiss Joan. I gasped loudly, my mouth dropped.

Candace came towards me as if to calm me, but I strode right past her. As I got to Joan, I saw a hickey on her neck. I looked at Candace, she was shaking her head "no" but I couldn't hear a thing. All I could hear was the sound of the ocean raging in my ears. I swear I saw red. I raised my fist and punched Joan awkwardly on the side of her head. She was more skilled and punched me back dead in my eye. And then we were fighting. The bell had rung and girls were pouring out of their classes. They started yelling and somebody was blowing a whistle. I just tried to hit her as many times as I could as hard as I could. I was screaming at her, "Keep your fucking hands off my girlfriend, you fucking bitch." I screamed it over and over again, even as it got quiet in the hallway, even as two teachers pulled us apart, even as Candace, mortified and frightened, backed away from me and ran the other way. That was the last time I saw her.

I got suspended for a week. My parents were embarrassed and disappointed and at a loss as to what to say to me. They were stunned when they heard what the fight was about and I think they were questioning themselves about what they must have done wrong. I had a terrible black eye, a swollen lip, and was sore all over. Everybody at school knew that I was a lesbian. Everybody knew that Candace was a lesbian. Everybody already knew that Joan was a lesbian, but now they thought she was some kind of girl-stealer as well. Viv said it was causing a lot of arguing and name-calling at school. People were starting to look at her funny too. There were not a lot of people who were sympathetic to me. But worst of all, Candace would not have anything to do with me. Her mom had her immediately transferred to another high school. I was beyond devastated.

It was the worst Christmas holiday and New Year's ever. Everybody was mad at me and embarrassed because of me. My sister was getting teased because of me. My black eye served as a constant reminder of my fight. We were not sure how the suspension would affect my college applications. It was a time fraught with stress and regret and shame. I spent New Year's Eve in my room listening to my love mix tape and crying. I re-read *The Color Purple* and cried.

When we got back to school in January, I was an outcast. Most of my old friends shunned me; they didn't want anybody thinking that about them too. I understood. I got a lot of disgusted looks, some threatening looks, and some pitying looks. I tried to ignore it all. I got bumped into a lot. I kept walking. Joan pointedly ignored me. Only Viv stayed by my side. A few girls I didn't know reached out to me and I was grateful. But I didn't want them to be touched by my problems, so I quietly ignored their attempts at friendship and they eventually gave up and faded away. I wrote Candace, but all the letters were returned unopened. I tried to call her. Either her mother or one of her sisters answered and told me not to call again. Denise, who had been my closest ally in the family, cursed me out and called me "nasty." Eventually, they had their number changed. I waited outside her church, across the street, watching for an opportunity to talk to her, but her family stayed close and I never saw her alone. I had Vivian talk to Candace for me. In no uncertain terms, she wanted nothing to do with me. Viv said she looked miserable, but it was little comfort. I spent what should have been the best time of my life—

spring of my senior year in high school—alone, sad and bereft. I sat in my room with my Walkman on and listened to Tracy Chapman and Phyllis Hyman over and over again. I did not go to prom. I finished school. I graduated summa cum laude but there was no joy in it, just relief. I was accepted at Yale University, now my first choice, and I decided to go there. Nobody else I knew was going there. I could start over. That summer, I received a letter from Candace.

Dear Dee,

I just want you to know that you have ruined my life. Your stupid jealous rage <u>has</u> made me an outsider in my own family. No one treats me the same anymore. I thought we were true friends, true loves (remember that!). But a friend would never have destroyed my life the way you did. I NEVER cheated on you, no matter what you think. You should have trusted me. Now I can never trust you again. Please don't call me or try to contact me again. We are over.
Sincerely,
Candace

The pain from that flat-out rejection was keen and I thought I would die of it. And though I may have welcomed it at that time, I didn't die. I packed up. And in the fall, I began my life again in college, without Candace.

CHAPTER EIGHTEEN

And so the summer of Dee and Noema began. New romance is always exciting and ours is no different. Noema and I both have busy lives, so we continue to "date" which keeps things interesting. We have lots of fun going out to eat, catching matinee movies and roller-skating. We go to NYC for a Broadway show, Rehoboth Beach for a weekend, and to the casinos to play craps, which she is unnaturally good at. We cook at each other's houses and meet each other's friends. The sex is great and we always have a lot to talk about. It is a great summer for me. I hardly think about Candace at all. Hardly.

Viv, on the other hand, started to break under the pressure of her failing relationship and finally gave in to cheating just to put an end to the suffering. She was kicked out, but she already had her plane ticket and plans, so it was just a few days that she needed to crash with friends. I was so happy that she came to stay with me for one of the last weekends in August. She came in on the Chinatown bus on a Friday night. I picked her up and we went out to eat right there in Chinatown. I got to catch her up on my summer and she told me all about her Cali plans.

"So you already have a place in Sherman Oaks? That's great Viv. I really hope you love it out there. I'm sure Cali will love you," I say. "I'm gonna miss not having you close though. I got used to it these past few months."

"Yeah, but now you have a place to visit, if you ever get any more vacation time, that is," she laughs. "Don't fret, *mon frère*, we have our cell phones, e-mail, Facebook, and if I really need to see you, I'll Skype you."

"True," I sigh. My text alert goes off again. "I guess I should check that." It is Noema, for the fourth time. Even though I told her all week that I would be hanging with my best friend tonight, she wanted to know where I was. I texted her back that I was at dinner. She wanted to know where. I tapped, "Chinatown." She wanted to know which restaurant; I texted, "Why?" She writes back that she wants to meet Viv tonight. I text back, "No, tomorrow, babe." Viv raises her eyebrows. I shrug, "She's just excited to meet you, that's all." Viv tilts her head and raises her eyebrows. "No seriously," I say. "She's cool. You'll love her. We're good together, really good together. I don't want to say, but I think this could be it. I think I already love her. She's smart, funny, beautiful, caring, artistic, and obviously, she has questionable taste in women," Viv continues. She laughs. "Seriously though, don't you think you might be jumping into this a smidge fast? Just a smidge?"

I think about it. "No," I say emphatically, "looking for Candace was just the closure I needed to be able to move on into adult relationships. I can imagine a future with Noema. I don't think I was ever able to do that before."

"OK, Dee. Well, I'm glad I'll get to meet her before I leave."

After we leave the restaurant, we bar hop then go home and crash. The next morning, we putz around listening to old school rap and eating cereal. We are not meeting Noema until dinner. Viv decides to visit her family before she's off to Cali so I drive her to her sister's place and wish her luck. Her family is crazy. I promise to be ready to pick her up at any time. I call Noema to see where she wants to go for dinner, but she doesn't pick up. Whatever! I hope she's over her ridiculousness. I really want her and Viv to get along. I wonder where she is. I stop along Kelly Drive. It is too muggy to run, but I love just sitting out here. I think the river soothes my soul.

BBBRRRrrriinggg!!! Oh no, not now! "Hello, this is Dee."

"Dee, it's time! Aragghhr!" says my only 36-week term teenage patient.

"Tina, how far apart are the contractions?" I ask, looking at my watch.

"Just five minutes Aarrrrgghhh! Whhoohhhahaaa!!"

"That was NOT five minutes!" I yell, running for my car.

"Where are you? Who's with you?"

"I was watching a *Twilight* movie at my sister's house. I wanted to finish it," she pants. Seriously?

"Are you close to the center?" I ask, trying to start my car and back out.

"No, I'm in Roxborough . . . Arrrrruuughghgh!!!"

"You don't have time ... get to the Roxborough Hospital, give them my name, and tell them I'm on my way. Don't you let them give you anything until I get there, OK? I'm only five minutes away!" I speed off.

Two hours later, Tina has a pink chubby healthy baby girl, but Tina is not doing well. Her blood pressure is way too high and she's a little disoriented. I decide to stay with her. Dinner will have to wait. I call Viv in the hallway.

"Where the hell are you? I told you to be ready. My sister and her husband are fighting, the kids are all out of the house, and my mother still refuses to come and talk to me. I walked over and saw my grandmother. I'm ready to get the hell out of here," she exclaims loudly.

"Yeah, Viv, I'm sorry about this but one of my patients went into labor and although she's already had the baby, I'm worried about her. She doesn't look right to me and I don't trust this hospital," I whisper. "I have to stay here a while."

"Shit, Dee!"

"I know, and I'm sorry. I've got two good options. One: You can take a cab to Main Street, I can get Noema to cab it up to Main Street and I can meet you guys for dinner. It's close enough that I can get back to the hospital if she needs me. Or two: you can cab down to South Philly and you and Noema can have the dinner we planned without me, just bring me back some food," I say.

"Boo to number one and hell no to number two. Damn, Dee! I wanted to change my clothes before dinner. OK, I'll meet you somewhere on Main Street. I'll let you know where I am when I get there. Good luck with your girlfriend, though," she says and hangs up.

I call Noema and explain the situation. She's as sweet as pie and agrees to meet us on Main Street. I hang up feeling relieved. Now to check on Tina....

Two hours later, Tina is stabilized and her family has finally shown up, so I leave the hospital and drag myself into one of the fanciest spots on Main Street. I look haggard; why didn't they pick the café down the block? Viv and Noema look halfway through their dinners and they are laughing and joking up a storm. Viv has always known how to flatter a girl and Noema loves the attention. I can see other patrons looking at them a little annoyed, but I am ecstatic. They are getting along! That's all I wanted. I kiss them both hello, sit down, and motion to the waiter.

"Jack and Coke and a menu, please," I say. The night passes pleasantly even though I smell like hospital.

After taking Noema home, I ask Viv what she thinks about her.

"I think she's seems cool enough. She was a lot of fun, but she's definitely a woman who will get what she wants. Originally, I was at that hip little café down the street but she insisted that we go somewhere "more private." I was fine and happy at the café but she would not be convinced. She wouldn't even sit down," Viv says.

"That's weird, usually she's very laid-back," I say, thoughtful.

"Could have just been me," Viv purrs. "I do have that effect on women." We laugh. I'm going to miss her. A lot.

I spend two nights with Noema that week. I admit I might have missed her a bit. I've gotten used to her voice, her touch, and her awesome *café au lait*. But I know I'll be busy next weekend and I don't want her to feel neglected. This coming weekend is Labor Day weekend, also known as Bernie's Bachelorette Extravaganza Weekend. Originally, her sister Beverly wanted to fly everyone out to Las Vegas, but none of us could commit to such a long trip, not even Bernie. So now, via chartered limo of course, we're going to a day spa, then a light dinner downtown, and then we're off to a club for naked boy dancing. It took over two weeks of e-mails and texts to come up with this final plan. Beverly is very intense about things being perfect. I am less than enthused, but I'm happy to see Bernie. She's been busy all summer, as have I, and we have a lot of catching up to do.

In the sage green 'gathering room,' we six women have stripped to our spa robes and slippers and are getting facials. I snag a lounger next to the bride and lie back to relax. The cool sound of Native American pipes wafts through the room as we collectively sigh and unwind. The very light and airy *pinot grigio* did its work too. The music reminds me briefly of Kokopelli and New Mexico, mountains and sky, but I push that thought away almost as soon as it arrives. I'm getting very good at that. I hear Bernie sigh next to me.

"How are you doing, sis?" I ask.

"Ah, well. I'm excited about the wedding itself. I do think it will be beautiful and fun. I'm so glad I hired a coordinator." I hear someone sucking their teeth on the other side of the room. "Whatever, Beverly! I wanted a professional and I won't keep apologizing for it!" she yells at her sister.

We hear mumbling, "Whatever, your wedding…outsider…so unnecessary." Then, "I know, sis, as long as you are happy!!!" in Beverly's sing-songy voice. Bernie sighs again.

To me she says, "But I'm stressed about work and life in general. I was really looking forward to today. Just a day with my friends to relax and have some fun."

I decide not to talk about my life, not now. Today is for Bernie. I exhale and let the spa work its magic on me.

Bernie gets her wish and the day goes really well. I'll even give Beverly some credit for it. The spa was perfect and everyone loved it. We had dinner at Buddhakan on Chestnut Street. The vibe was fun and casual, the food was great, the drinks were even better. I got to know Bernie's other friends and everyone was getting along great. By 9:00 p.m., it was time to say goodbye to the big golden Buddha and hello to some big, black, naked men. I really thought that as professional women, we would be skipping this kind of entertainment, but Beverly liked to be thorough and her only sister was going to have the full bachelorette experience. As usual, she came prepared with 100 one-dollar bills in her purse, as well as a stash of antibacterial wipes.

When we get out of the limo and look at this "strip club," I think we all have the same thought: "What the hell are we doing here?" But then we turn the corner and see the line of patiently waiting, well-heeled women snaking down the block and then I'm pretty sure it was just me still thinking, "What the hell am I doing here?" My companions start to get a hungry look about them. Some get loud and boisterous; some get quiet, lick their lips, and stare off into space. Even Bernie looks unnaturally intense. I sidle up to her as we shuffle forward in line.

"What's up, sis?" I ask. "Not your cup of tea? Or did you arrange this part yourself?' I tease, but she's not up for teasing. She's thinking deep thoughts.

"I was just thinking. I haven't been with anybody but Darryl in five years and now, I am committing myself to NEVER being with anybody else, again, EVER," she says.

"Yup, that just about sums it up. You get to play tonight, though," I offer.

"Yes, but what if it just makes me want someone else? Forever is a long time, Dee," she says.

"Yeah, but you love, Darryl. You've been in love with him since your first tutoring session together. You two are perfect for each other. You won't want anyone else, don't worry," I console.

She looks at me quizzically. "Dee, that sounds awfully romantic of you. What's going on? Are you seeing somebody?" she asks. Damn, she knows me too well.

"I am. It's new, but it's good. Real good," I say. I smile and blush.

"Well, now. That's good news. Well, I want to hear all about her, another time, though. Tonight we're having fun! What happens in the club stays in the club, right?" she asks. We're next in line. We pull out our IDs as Beverly waves us through.

"Absolutely!" I enthuse, "Let's see what these guys got going on!"

Now, what's a gay woman to do at a male strip club? Well, I drink my usual, I enjoy the eye candy – those guys put on a good show. I drink some more and I almost pee myself watching Bernie and Beverly up on stage getting humped doggie-style. I, myself, even get a sweet lap dance by the cutest dancer of the night. His ass is truly outstanding! But mostly, I flirt with the sexy waitress. She started it – leaning over with all her cleavage in my face, whispering in my ear, sitting on my lap, and bringing me a free drink. I know she's probably a dancer and I know she's probably just trying to get more tips. I also know she just might be bored but there is a lot of sexual energy flying around that room and she is hot. So when she follows me to the ladies room, I'm not surprised. She steers me past the door to a little hallway off to the side.

"Hi," she says as she slinks towards me. I back up slowly.

"Hi, yourself," I reply, finally feeling the wall on my back.

"I've been thinking about you all night," she says, unbuttoning her blouse.

"Me? I bet you say that to all the girls," I stammer. She's already taken my hand and put it on her breast. She's fast!

"No, not all the girls, only the sexy ones," she purrs and kisses my neck.

I pull my hand away. "I can't," I protest, "I have a girlfriend." She presses up against me thrusting her muscular thigh between my legs. A moan escapes me. My hand impulsively reaches down to feel her naked ass under her mini skirt.

"But you want to and she never has to know." She grinds on me and puts my hand back on her breast. She turns up her face to kiss me.

"As sexy as you are and as much as I want you right now, I can't do this." I retrieve my hands and gently slide away from her. "She might not ever know, but I would." I break away from her spell and walk back to the bright restroom sign exhaling shakily. I can hear her suck her teeth behind me. She avoids me the rest of the night, which is OK by me, but I don't think I would be strong enough to resist her a second time.

The night ends well. Everyone seems happy and satisfied. Those dancers worked Bernie out, but I can tell it was more cathartic than confusing and she looks content. Beverly had delivered on a very successful bachelorette party. She looked mighty pleased with herself as she received her accolades in the limo at the end of the night. I went to Noema's place. After that waitress, I had some unfinished business to tend to, and she was the delighted recipient of all that entailed.

September flies by fast. Work has picked up some, although Soledad is considering retiring and that is causing some stress at the office. I can't imagine not seeing her everyday, not hearing her lilting accent when she curses out some insurance agent.

And then there's Noema. We are both very busy, but we make time for each other and it has been good … really good … surprisingly good. Noema has somehow slid into my life and become my regular jawn without me even realizing it. One day, we're just dating, the next, she's keeping some clothes at my house. Today, she's insisting that I come as her date to a party. Although I prefer to keep my practice and my personal life separate, just this time, for Noema, I will go to Laurie and Leslie's baby shower.

CHAPTER NINETEEN

Although babies are my bread and butter (a little midwifery joke there), I am feeling a bit overwhelmed by all these major life moments happening around me. Everyone seems to be taking that next step, and I feel like I'm on the sidelines. I watch Noema get dolled up for the shower and wonder if she will be the reason for any next step I take. She catches me looking at her and strikes a pose. I laugh and wonder, "Could she be the one?"

The shower is at Laurie and Leslie's house, a large newly renovated townhouse in East Falls. It's a beautiful sunny Saturday and as we head down Kelly Drive to their house, I can't help but wish I were out there running instead. Babies are my thing, baby showers are not. After 10 minutes, we finally find parking but have to lug our huge stroller in a box for three blocks. I suggest we take it out and roll it; she gives me the slant eye. We get to the house and it is packed. Both Laurie and Leslie have large supportive families and a ton of friends. I am wondering how this is going to be any fun at all if I can't even breathe. We greet the couple. Of course, I just saw them on Tuesday, but this is different. They announce that I am their midwife and I am immediately swamped with people who want to talk to me about the baby and impending birth, etc. I lose Noema to her own group of friends and just surrender to talking shop the whole afternoon.

I finally hook back up with Noema about 40 minutes later when lunch is served. She seems a little distracted. Over my plate and gulping some white wine out of a plastic cup, I ask her, "What's wrong babe?"

"Oh, nothing," she says. She picks at her food for a minute but then sees a friend.

"Hey, Syreeta! Come here and meet Dee." Syreeta, a plump light-skinned woman with knee-length locks and a nose ring, squeezes through to greet us.

"Ah, the infamous Dee! I'm so happy to meet you. I've heard a lot about you," she says with a warm smile.

"Hello," I say, "I hope it's been all good." I look to smile at Noema but she's looking past me.

"Excuse me," Noema says getting up. "You two get to know each other, I have to see about something…." And she took her leave of us. I shrugged, Syreeta shrugged and took Noema's seat and we chatted. Thankfully, there is no game playing, but we do have to open gifts and that just about killed me! One hundred onesies, 10 bath gift baskets, five copies of *Goodnight, Moon*, and after 45 minutes, I couldn't take it anymore and went to go look for Noema. She had missed them opening our stroller. Maybe something was wrong.

I found her in a sparsely decorated office space next to the garage having a heated discussion with a woman I'd never seen before. The woman was impressive. She wore a tailored suit, sported a baldie, and had an air of unmistakable confidence about her. She was looking very serious and determined.

"Hello," I say to the woman, and then I turn to Noema. "Hey babe, I don't mean to interrupt, but they opened our stroller and you missed it." I was aware that I sounded petty and whiny, but I was a little thrown off.

"I did? Oh, sorry. Dee, this is Danny, an old friend of mine." Danny snorts, reaches across and gives me a limp handshake.

"How you doing?" she says.

"Good, good, and yourself?" I ask politely.

"Peachy," she says sarcastically and turns slightly away from me.

I turn to Noema and give her a questioning look. She shrugs it off.

"I'll be up in a few minutes. I just want to finish this conversation first, OK?" she says sweetly, dismissing me.

"OK," I say and walk away slowly, thinking it was odd but not worrying too much. Noema loved me and I trusted her. She would tell me what that was all about later. But she didn't. The day was too hectic, and that night we went out to Marlene's with another group of her friends for the shower "after party." She had some work to do early on Sunday and then the week was really busy, and eventually, I just forgot about it.

Thank goodness none of my patients were close to labor because Bernie's wedding was just two weeks away and I was plunged into the whirlwind of that – final dress fittings, phone calls from a nervous Bernie, phone calls from an anxious Beverly, the rehearsal, the rehearsal dinner, and finally the wedding day. The ceremony itself was at 3:00 p.m. in a beautiful old church on the Main Line. The morning of the wedding was long and tiring – the bridesmaids breakfast, the salon, and then back to her parents' house for make-up and dressing. We would not go to the actual church until it was time to walk down the aisle. Beverly didn't want anybody to see Bernie before the wedding, so we holed up in her mom's house drinking white wine spritzers and trying to relax and not get bored.

"Dee," says Bernie, lounging in her slip, "tell me about your new girlfriend. I'm tired of thinking about me and Darryl and "our love." I want to hear about someone else, OK?"

"Well, her name is Noema, she's from New Orleans but moved up after she graduated from the Moore College of Art. She's a little younger than me, than us, but she's a great artist and does pretty well for herself," I oblige.

"OK, that's her resume. Tell me about *her*. I want the juicy stuff," says Bernie sipping her spritzer.

"Well, you'll see her at the reception, but she's beautiful, tall with a lot of hair, nose ring, and a big tattoo on her back. I think she's wearing a red dress today, so you won't miss her."

"Ooh, red at a wedding! She's bold, I like it!" enthuses Bernie.

"Actually, for an artist, she's incredibly level-headed. She's very focused on getting her new show together. She's been spending a lot of time at her studio working on getting the pieces just right for it," I explain.

Bernie sighs. "Boring! Dee, you sound like an old married lady already. Tell me the good stuff. How's the sex? What's the craziest date you two have ever had? I need distraction! I'm starting to sweat."

"All right already. Let's see. The sex. It's good. It was wild and crazy when we first started dating, we did it just about anywhere, in my car, in a bathroom stall at Marlene's, on my balcony...." I laugh when Bernie gasps. "Did I mention she belly dances?"

"Oh, I like this girl," she says. "So do you love her or is this just another fling?"

"I ... I think this might be something. We get along really well; we both have odd work schedules so that kind of makes things easier, she's fun, she's got a good heart. I really dig her. It might just go somewhere, we'll see.... But let's just get you married first."

Bernie laughs. "I'm so happy for you, Dee! I remember when Darryl and I first fell in love, it was so exciting and wonderful and it's like you can't believe it's actually happening to you, everything they write about in romance novels, you feel it. Of course, with me, Darryl was my first love, so I was blessed. God just brought him straight to me when I was ready, when Darryl was ready, and it all just fell into place." Bernie sighs and finally looks relaxed.

"Yeah, you and Darryl are definitely blessed."

The wedding is beautiful. Bernie floats down the aisle to Darryl who is wiping away tears. The whole ceremony is lively and celebratory, sincere and meaningful, but full of love and hope and joy. I think that it is the perfect wedding and I am full of love and longing. I glance at Noema sitting in the back; she looks mesmerized with tearful eyes. I'm so glad we are on the same page. The reception is elegant without being stuffy and we have a lot of fun at our table. Noema and I are the only lesbian couple there, but we don't sweat it. Darryl's cousin John is there with his partner, so we hang out with them a bit, trading dance partners and quips. When we go home, we make love slowly. She looks so gorgeous in her dress, I don't take it completely off. There's something about a woman in a red dress and pumps. Afterwards, I hold her and tell her I love her. She kisses me into silence.

❧ CHAPTER TWENTY ❧

BBBRRRrrriinnnngggg!!! I'm catching up on *Grey's Anatomy* when I get the call.

"Hello, this is Dee," I say calmly.

"Dee, this is Leslie." Her warm, rich voice is edged with adrenaline. "I think it's time. I've timed the contractions and they are exactly five minutes apart. She passed her mucous plug a few hours ago and we've been walking and dancing to pass the time. But now, it's time," she says.

"OK. I'll meet you guys at the center in 15 minutes. Can I speak to Laurie, first though please?" I ask.

"Sure!" She hands the phone over to Laurie and I hear shuffling about.

"Hi," says Laurie in her sweet voice. "I've been contracting all day, Dee, since about 2:00 p.m. I'm so excited. I can't wait to meet this little baby. I love that I am exactly 40 weeks today, Dee; she is right on time! Hey, can you tell Noema that we're in labor, she wanted to come right after the baby is born."

"Sure, I'll call her. She's at the studio working," I say.

"She is? Oh, oh, oh, aaaahhhhhhhh…." I hear her pant her way through the contraction. Good. She's handling it.

"Laurie, you're doing great. That was great breathing. Did your water break? Do you feel any pressure near your bottom?"

"No, no water, no pressure, just the contractions, which hurt like hell, by the way," she replies cheerfully.

"Good. Just keep breathing. I'll see you guys in a few minutes. Please tell Leslie to drive sensibly. You do not want to have an accident!!! OK? You have time," I caution.

"OK, see you there! Bye bye now," Laurie says breathlessly.

I get my bag and call Noema on my way out the door. When she picks up, she sounds breathless too. I can hear music in the background.

"Hi," I say. "I just called to tell you that Laurie is in labor and that we are headed to the birth center. I'll call you when the baby arrives, OK?"

"OK. Thanks for the call." And she hangs up. That was weirdly detached, but maybe she's really into her work.

When I arrive at the center, Laurie and Leslie are heading inside with their bags. Tracy Ann has unlocked the door for them. My birth assistant, Beth, is also there and the OBs have been notified. I follow Laurie and Leslie back to the bigger birthing room and we get set up. Beth has already turned up the heat, turned on the electric candles, and started the Jacuzzi. I show Leslie where the sound system is and she plugs in her iPod and pulls up her labor playlist. Soothing piano fills the room and I think we all exhale at the same time. Then she plugs in a lavender-scented oil diffuser and lays out a snack table of trail mix and water bottles. Laurie is slowly pacing around the room in a walking rocking motion. I wash my hands, put on my scrubs, double check the room for supplies and pull Laurie's chart and birthing plan. I go over it and take it to Laurie. She checks it and nods. She wants an all-natural birth with as little interference as necessary. I will do my best to make this happen for her. I check her vitals and then check her progress. She's 5 cm dilated. A few minutes later, Laurie's mother and sister come into the room, everyone washes their hands and hugs hello. We will be the circle of women who bring this child forward.

In 15 minutes, I have Laurie change so that she can get into the Jacuzzi when she is ready. Her contractions are about four minutes apart, but she is handling them well. I monitor her blood pressure and make sure she stays hydrated. Her family is talking softly, encouraging her, making gentle jokes, talking to each other. In another 45 minutes, her contractions are about three minutes apart and she can no longer talk through them. I lay her down for an examination. She is about 7 cm dilated and her bag is still intact. I suggest she try the Jacuzzi and she agrees. I relax on my stool while her family helps her into the giant tub. She breathes out and relaxes.

Laurie, who is normally so bubbly and outgoing, has gone inside herself. I can see her communing with her body and I know she will be fine. Leslie is visibly anxious. I have her hand out snacks and water to everyone. She also takes some pictures. An hour later, Laurie is ready to get out of the tub. After she dries off, I do another examination. She's 9 cm now and the contractions are coming every minute or so. We gather in a circle and say a prayer. A flute plays. We separate and get ready to help Laurie go through transition. It hits her and she shouts through her next few contractions. Leslie winces but holds Laurie on the yoga ball as she rolls and rocks on it. They walk, they dance, and they hold each other up. I think even Laurie's mother is moved by their devotion to each other. Laurie's water finally breaks around 2:00 a.m. and she yells at the next contraction. I check her; she's ready to push. I bring out the birthing stool.

Laurie gets settled onto the stool. I take my place at her side and massage her calves. The birth assistant gets the bassinet ready for the baby. We dim the lights. We laugh as Leslie dashes to change the music, time for the pushing playlist! When Salt-N-Pepa's "Push it" comes on, we all crack up and almost miss Laurie's contraction. Luckily she doesn't and pushes through the laughter. Laurie has been waiting for this moment for nine long months and three years of trying before that. She's ready. She pushes that baby steadily down and 10 minutes later the head starts to crown. Another two pushes and that beautiful baby slides right out into Leslie's (and my) hands.

"It's a girl!" I exclaim the obvious and can't stop my own tears. Nobody notices me as they are crying themselves. Laurie and Leslie are kissing and crying and laughing all at the same time. It was truly a beautiful birth. As Laurie holds the baby, we deliver the placenta and I clean up around this new family. I do my work meticulously, staying alert for trouble as I take care of my patients. I am humbled by the ongoing miracle of life and feel blessed to be able to do what I do. Every birth reaffirms my reason for existence. I say silent prayers for this family as I always do and retreat so they can begin their life together. They name the baby Lola Mae and she is perfection.

After breastfeeding and napping, when Lola is sleeping, I slip off for a shower and a nap in the "midwives' quarters." It's 7:00 a.m. and sunny when I awake. As I walk down the hall, I hear a familiar voice and smile. Through the small window, I see Noema holding the baby and cooing. I hesitate as I see that behind her is the woman from the baby shower. She's leaning over to see the baby, but she's got her hands casually on Noema's waist. As I slowly open the door, everyone looks up at me. Noema opens her mouth in surprise, Leslie and Laurie look instantly worried, and the woman defiantly looks right at me and keeps her hands on Noema.

"Hello?" I say.

"Oh, hi. I thought you would be back home by now," says Noema.

"No, I stayed over so I could keep an eye on my patients," I say coolly, eyeing the other woman. Leslie calmly walks over and takes the baby from Noema. I look at her but she looks away guiltily.

"Could we have some privacy?" I say to Noema and her friend. "I need to examine Laurie now."

"Sure, of course. We'll be outside," Noema says to Laurie. She and the woman walk out together. I do my best to hold my tongue. I shake off my indignation and throw on the cloak of professionalism and do a quick but thorough examination of Laurie. She's fine. I check the baby in Leslie's arms. She looks good. I ask about the breastfeeding and suggest they put her right back on to feed. I smile at Laurie.

"You were really exceptional last night. You did everything perfectly. You remember Meadow, right? She'll be here in a couple of hours, I'll stay until she gets here but she will do your next exam, OK?" I say.

"OK." She says and takes the baby to feed her. I start to leave but Leslie puts her hand on my shoulder.

"Dee, I'm sorry about this. I don't know what is going on…." she starts, but I stop her.

"You don't owe me an explanation here, Leslie. This has nothing to do with you," I say. I'm trying to steel myself to walk through the door and see my girlfriend with that other woman. My thoughts are in a jumble and I just want to get out of there. Then I remember there is another exit through the bathroom. I take it without another thought.

I bypass the waiting room and slip into my office where I wait for the workday to begin for the rest of the office. I'm numb, but I try to think. Am I overreacting? OK, what did I see? They were just looking at the baby, close, but they had to be to get a good look, right? Maybe Leslie and Laurie just happened to invite them both over at the same time. Maybe it's all a big misunderstanding. Maybe I'm being ridiculous, jealous and petty over nothing. Should I call her? Maybe text her? I can't just run away. This is my job, my office, and my territory. Why did she bring her here? OK, I need to make a decision…. but before I can call Noema, she calls me.

"Hello?" I say shakily.

"Dee. Maybe we should talk," says Noema on the other line. My heart sinks.

"I guess so." I whisper.

"Can you talk today? I know you had a long night but what about over dinner? I'll come to your house," she says very efficiently.

"No, how about in a couple of hours at your house? I won't be sleeping or eating until I know what the hell is going on," I confess.

"OK," she says, "I'll meet you at my house at 10:00 a.m." As I open my mouth to ask the question swirling around my mind, "Why?" she ends the call. I stare at my cluttered desk. Kokopelli, the trickster, seems to be laughing into his flute.

❧

I ring her buzzer at 10:00 a.m. on the dot. She buzzes me in and I walk the long flights up to get to her door. In the past few months, I've been flying up the stairs two at a time. But this morning, it takes all my strength just to keep stepping up, one at a time. She opens the door when I get there and lets me inside. No hug, no kiss, she just shows me to the kitchen table where she's put out coffee and danish. How very fucking civilized of her. It's insulting, but I'm trying to keep an open mind because truly I do not understand what the hell is going on.

My girlfriend opens her mouth to speak.

"Dee, I'm really sorry. I…I've been seeing Danny." She looks down.

"What do you mean? Who is she? You're seeing her? If you weren't happy ... I thought we ... I thought we were happy." I am numb and just blown away.

Noema takes a deep breath and says, "Dee, I should have told you about her before. I'm really sorry. Danny and I have been off and on for about five years. We had broken up again when she had to go work in London this summer, when you and I ..."

What the hell! "Wait, are you telling me that you were already in a relationship when we started dating?" I ask.

"No, like I said, it's been off and on, we fight a lot and she travels a lot and I just wanted a normal relationship and you are so great and beautiful and smart. I never thought that it would actually get this far...."

My mouth is open. "Wait. All this time, I thought we were getting serious about each other. I love you, Noema. I love being with you, I think that we are great together, don't you?"

"Well, yes, of course I do. I love being with you too, I just thought it would be more of a summer fling, but then you were so great and then Danny came home and then honestly, I didn't know what to do. I didn't want to hurt you."

Like a broken record I repeat, "Wait. Are you saying that you are with her now? How long has she been here?"

"She came back the end of August, the same weekend your friend came in town."

"August! What the fuck!? Have you been cheating on me since August? It's October! I *can't*. Why did you lie to me all this time??"

"I didn't lie, exactly. I was not with her when we met, and I wasn't sure what would happen with her and me. And you were so busy with wedding stuff, I didn't want to ruin it for you. I'm so sorry," she says.

I try to take it all in; my mind is reeling. "Has this been a game to you? Why was Leslie trying so hard to fix me up with you if she knew you already had somebody?"

She laughs, "Leslie has always hated Danny. She thought I should be with somebody nicer, more stable. She thinks the world of you, you know."

"So all this time, I thought we were in a real relationship, maybe headed towards a future together and you thought I was a summer fling, somebody just to spend time with until she came back home? Are you serious?" I am angry, I am shocked, I am bamboozled, I am tricked, I am speechless. I stand up. How could I have been so stupid?

I say, "I just want you to know that I really loved you. I did, and I thought you felt the same. I cannot believe that you are so heartless and such a liar. You are not the woman I thought you were, not at all."

She tears up and nods. She inclines her head towards a box by the door. It is full of my things. Unfuckingbelievable.

"I am really sorry," she says and looks uncertain. "I didn't mean for it to get this far. I didn't mean to hurt you, Dee." She reaches her hand out to me but I step back out of reach.

"I … never mind…. Good-bye, Noema." I pick up my box and walk out the door. I do not let my tears come until I am safely in my car and driving up Fifth Street.

I get home and as soon as I put the box down, I don't want to be there. It reminds me of Noema. I'm tired as hell but I change into sweats, grab my running shoes and head back out the door. It's the end of October and it's chilly, but the sun is still shining bright and the leaves are turning colors and the rest of the world is going about it's normal routine, oblivious to my upended life and heartbreak. I get to Kelly Drive and start running. Running and thinking. Running and stopping to catch my breath, running and stopping to drink from the public water fountain (yuck!), running and jumping over goose poop. I just want to run.

I try to piece together everything Noema said with my vision of our relationship. How could she be so cruel? How could I be so stupid? How could we be in the same relationship and yet so far apart? Exhausted and more pissed than sad, I look at my watch. I have to go and check on Laurie. I'm not sure I want to face them, but it's my job. I decide to go straight to the birth center. I can shower and change there.

I slip in the birth center, grab an extra set of clothes from my office, take a quick shower, and then pop in to see Laurie and Leslie. Laurie is asleep and Leslie is sitting in the rocker with Lola. She looks up at me and frowns.

"How's Laurie?" I ask.

"She's great, a little tired but Lola just finished nursing, so she's gonna get some rest. You're not going to wake her, are you?" she asks protectively.

"No." I check the chart. The nurse changed her bedding an hour ago, Meadow has seen her twice today, and she looks peaceful. I'll let her sleep. She's going to need it.

"How are you doing? Have you gotten some sleep yet?" I ask Leslie.

"Oh, a little. I'm too wired to sleep though. I can't believe our daughter is here. She's so beautiful, she's so perfect. Thank you," she says to me.

"Well, I just helped, you guys did all the hard work and you have a lot of hard work ahead of you, But from what I see, you'll handle it just fine," I say truthfully.

"I'm sorry about Noema," she says. "I thought she was done with that person. I really did. And you are so nice and smart and sweet and cool and beautiful. I thought you would be perfect together. I love Noema a lot; she's like a sister to me but I don't understand why she keeps going back to that person."

"So you knew about that? Great. Look, it's not your fault; she's a grown woman and made her own choices, as did I. I just wish … Listen, I'm gonna go. When Laurie wakes up, buzz me. I'll examine her and then sign your discharge papers. Since Lola is asleep, you should try to rest, too. OK?"

"OK. I did want to thank you again for the birth. It was perfect, exactly what we wanted for the beginning of our little girl's life," she says looking up at me. I take the baby from her and hold her gently.

I whisper into her tiny ear, "Lola Mae, you are a lucky little girl to have two such great mommies. May you always be so blessed. May you always be happy. May you always have wise guidance. May you always feel as loved as you are this moment." I give her back to Leslie and say, "You're very welcome." I walk out and feel the tears well up in my eyes. I feel jealous of that little girl, jealous of their family. But mostly I just feel a like a fool.

CHAPTER TWENTY-ONE

Sunday is Halloween. I decide to spend it at my parent's house giving out candy. I bring over some merlot and we eat an early dinner of chili and corn bread, and then wait for the trick or treaters. For fun, my sister and I decide to dress up like vampires. We sit on the porch swing, wrapped in capes, surrounded by tea lights with our goblets of red wine. The bucket of candy is at our feet. She asks me about Noema. I hesitate, then decide to tell her the whole story.

"Wow!" she says when I'm done.

"Yeah, wow," I repeat. "Can you believe what a pathological liar she turned out to be? How can you be in a relationship and never mention that you are also in a relationship with someone else? Broken up or not. Asshole!"

"Yeah, I would think that when you told her about Candace she would have at least mentioned that she was going through something similar," Janine says.

"Candace is a completely different situation. She and I have not been in a relationship since we were 17. Why would I tell her about that?" I snap.

"Whoa. You never told her that you had just spent months looking for your long lost first love?" asks my sister.

"No! It had nothing to do with her…or us. Shut up, Janine," I snap again and take a big gulp of my wine. I pull out my cell phone and call Noema. She picks up on the second ring.

"Yes?" she says warily.

"You lying bitch!" I whisper angrily into the phone. My sister makes a lunge for the phone and hits the 'end' button just as a group of five little kids walk up—a Transformer, a princess, a cowboy, a ninja, and Wonder Woman. I glare at Janine, and she gives me a "What the hell are you doing?" face.

"Trick or treat!!!"

We laugh, but after we give out the candy, I stumble into the house. I don't want to be happy.

❧

One day early in November, Leslie calls and asks if she can come over to get a few of Noema's things. I've had them boxed up for weeks just waiting to throw them in her face. But of course she's smart enough not to come herself.

"Sure," I sigh, "How about tonight? No time like the present, right?"

It's a Friday and I'm off work. I decide to go for a run on Kelly Drive. The chill in the air and the brown crispy leaves underfoot match my mood. I think about Noema constantly. I wonder how I could have been so wrong about our relationship. I wonder if she ever thinks about me. I wonder what is wrong with me. I try to run off the feeling of being unlovable, unpartnerable (is that a word?). I run and run and run, but the feeling remains. I drag myself back to my car and drive home.

I decide to make a final sweep of the place to make sure I got rid of everything. After walking through my apartment, making mental notes of all the things that we did there and there and there, I finally go into my sex drawer and decide to throw out all my toys. We used every single one of them and I remember exactly how she made me feel, exactly what her body felt like, exactly how she kissed, exactly how she came.

Leslie knocks softly on the door as if not to disturb a sleeping baby. But I have already stemmed the tide of my tears with a generous vodka and cranberry. And while I am listening to Marvin Gaye, I'm not really feeling nostalgic anymore. I'm feeling a little pissed off about the whole thing. Why does she think she should get her sweatshirts and face cleanser back? Fuck her! I get off the sofa to let in Leslie. She's wearing a button-down red blouse tucked into form-fitting gray slacks. She's dressed like she's just running an errand on her way home from work. I'm an errand. But she hugs me hello and I step into it and hold on. I'm a little wobbly.

"Hi," I say casually when we part.

"Hi, Dee. How are you doing?" she asks cautiously.

"Oh fine, you don't have to walk on eggshells with me." I wave my hand at her. "I'm just fine. How are Laura and Lola? I know you have pictures, let me see!"

I flop back onto the sofa and take another sip of my cocktail. She sits down next to me and pulls out her phone. She scrolls through picture after picture as I ooh and ahh. While she is telling me about the new pediatrician, a picture of Lola, Noema, and Danny slides into view. I suck in my breath and she hurriedly swipes to the next picture, but I don't even see it. My eyes blur and all I can see is the picture, their arms around each other's waists holding the baby in between, three happy, smiling faces.

"I'm so sorry, Dee, I forgot that was in here. I'm so sorry."

She puts the phone away.

"So they are together?" I ask. She nods and looks down.

"OK, that's OK, I knew it anyway, it's fine," I mumble and take another sip, trying shake off the idea of Noema and Danny.

Leslie takes my hand in consolation. She also starts mumbling about being sorry and how she feels responsible and she wishes she didn't get involved and all I can think about is the incredible warmth and power in her hand. I'm nodding at her, but my tears are drying up and I can see she's feeling better, more confident of my forgiveness, she's apologizing in earnest, looking into my eyes and thanking me for being such a good midwife. She is such a sincere woman. Her eyes are searching mine, looking for absolution, her hand is so strong, her palm so warm. I'm imagining her hand on me, on my back, pulling me closer. I look at her face so close to mine, I see her in minute detail; she is a fine, fine woman. Her voice washes over me. My emotions are numb but my body is beginning to ache for her touch. I slowly turn her hand in mine so that it rests on my thigh. I lean in and kiss her mid-sentence. Before our lips can touch I hear her surprised "Oh!" and she jumps up out of my grasp, breaking me out of my reverie.

Leslie is slowly backing up and repeating, "oh" and "sorry." I hear myself repeating her "oh" and "sorry" as I get up, but I don't exactly mean it. She bends down to pick up the box for Noema. I apologize again, gesture towards the glass, the box. She nods and says it's OK, but she looks disappointed in me.

I shut the door behind her. I pick up my glass, drain the watered down contents and leave it by the kitchen sink. I go to bed, masturbate to the memory of Leslie's voice, the feel of her strong warm hand, and then I cry myself to sleep.

CHAPTER TWENTY-TWO

I decide I need to cleanse my life, again. I rearrange my furniture – I need some new *feng shui*. I buy new sheets and bedding and towels. I actually read through some of the Iyanla Vanzant books. I consider joining a meditation group. But I am lonely.

I throw myself into work, which is pretty easy since I have seven births that month – the most ever for me. But I handle them all pretty well and it never gets old for me. Soledad announces that she's retiring next summer so we have time to hire a new midwife and get her up to speed. I'm grateful for the postponement; I don't want to see her go. Meadow has become somewhat of a superstar with her book coming out and business has picked up significantly. But I am lonely.

In a moment of desperation, I call Candace. My heart thumps while the phone rings and I gasp when I hear her voice. But it is only her voicemail message. I'm neither as prepared nor as smooth as I would like to be, but I leave a message anyway.

"Hi, Candace. This is Dee. I got your letter a few months ago and I totally respect your decision. I was just calling to see how you are doing. I don't know if this is possible, but I would really like to try and be friends again.

It was so good talking to you and I just miss that. I miss our friendship, so if you're willing and able, please give me a call back at this number."

I hang up and stare at the phone for a full 15 minutes. Nothing. I move on with my day. I have a lot of work to do, but I am lonely.

I spend my 32nd birthday at work. My co-workers take me out to TGIFridays. They are sweet to me. The wait staff sings "Happy Birthday" and I blow out the candle on my slice of chocolate cake. I go home with my co-workers' presents and I have lots of my cards from my family and friends on my mantle. I smile at them. I turn off the lights and walk into my bedroom. I turn on the news to drive away the sounds of me getting ready for bed, alone.

Thanksgiving arrives and I go to my parents with my macaroni and cheese and pumpkin pie. My sister is there with her new boyfriend, Joe, and my aunt is there with her son and his family. Dinner is great; we stuff ourselves, play Taboo afterwards and watch football. I drink beer with my dad. I talk to Viv that night on the phone. She loves California, but she's lonely too. I keep her from drunk-dialing Morgan. She keeps me from drunk-dialing Noema…again.

A few days later, Bernie calls me and invites me out to dinner. I gratefully accept.

We meet at a popular restaurant downtown. It is packed for their holiday happy hour. We find a corner table and order drinks. I order a Dark and Stormy.

"So, how's married life?" I ask.

"Surprisingly, just like our life before except now we are expected to host family gatherings and everyone keeps asking me about babies. What about you? How's Noema?"

I'd forgotten. I hadn't really talked to her in the last few months. So I took a big breath and told her the whole story of Noema.

"I'm so sorry, Dee. I really am. You seemed so hopeful about this one, different too. Like you were really ready to settle down," she says. I nod and sigh.

"There's more, too. I didn't want to bother you with my drama while you were getting ready for your wedding…but before I got with Noema, I went looking for Candace…." I end up telling her that whole story over dinner.

"Wow, Dee! Who knew you were such a romantic!" she says. "Well, damn! That is a lot of drama. What the hell? I just saw you in September! I'm so sorry. Sorry about both. Aww honey, that's a lot of heartbreak. How are you doing?" she asks, searching my eyes looking for signs of a breakdown.

"I'm…well, I was so let down after finding Candace. But then Noema was there and well, the Noema thing, that was great, at least I thought it was great, and then I just felt so betrayed – I was just so angry and sad, and now, now, I just feel drained and confused. I couldn't make it work with my old love, I couldn't make it work with my new love. Maybe I'm not supposed to be in love and have a partner like that. Maybe a midwife is all I get to be."

Bernie looked at me with so much sympathy and love, I felt even worse about everything. God, I was pathetic.

"You will, Dee. Have faith. Maybe they weren't the right women; maybe it wasn't the right time. Just get yourself ready for when that right person shows up. Have you gotten rid of all your baggage? Have you let go of all these hurts and heartbreaks? You have to make space for new love."

"But that's the thing, Bernie. I thought I did all that. I was open for Noema, I was ready for new love and I thought I'd found it and look what happened. She used me, she lied to me and she threw me away when her real woman showed up," I say.

"But didn't you just tell me you had been looking for Candace for months? Are you sure you were completely ready for Noema?"

"But that was different, I was just looking for Candace to see what happened to her and you know, if ... I was just nostalgic.... I remembered how we were and I wondered ... you know, if it was still there."

"And was it?"

"Actually, yeah. I think so. The love, the friendship, the attraction was still there, at least for me. But she chose her husband, so whatever, right? So I had to move on, and I did. And then Noema, that bitch, treated me like shit." With righteous indignation, I sit back hard in my chair and cross my arms.

"We're friends, right? I have to be able to say this to you. Dee, she treated you the way I've seen you treat other women. I hate to say it. You know I love you, but I've seen you be callous with other people's feelings, a little self-serving and inconsiderate," she says looking intently at me. I look out the window.

"So you think this is karma? You think I deserved all of this?" I ask Bernie.

"No! No, honey, that's not what I'm saying. I'm saying maybe being on the other side of hurt will help you be a better person," she says.

"But I've been hurt. I've been hurt plenty. This thing with Noema really knocked me back. And Candace broke up with me when we were kids, and then she rejected me again. And that hurt, a lot," I protest.

Bernie looks at me. "I know she broke up with you in high school, but from what you told me, wasn't that really your doing?"

"Perhaps I shouldn't have punched that girl," I say, looking out the window.

"Perhaps you should have trusted Candace," she retorts. "But that was high school, who knows anything at that age?"

"Yeah, but now we're grown and she's married and I'm an idiot," I say resignedly and finish my drink.

CHAPTER TWENTY-THREE

Christmas. At the office, we get lots of holiday cards with pictures of our babies in Santa hats and reindeer antlers. Their growth over a scant year or two never ceases to amaze me. We have our annual holiday party at a local restaurant. Spouses are invited but I don't even have a date. I am actually fine with this. I have gotten used to my own company again and, thankfully, I'm still cool with me. I rock my "Jackson Five Christmas Album," I buy myself a lovely turquoise necklace to go with my earrings, and I keep cinnamon-scented candles burning in my house. I have my own little tree that I decorate with mini disco balls and dancing lights and I am OK.

On Christmas Eve, I get a frantic call from Meadow. She's technically on call and one of our patients has gone into labor. But she is stuck in New Jersey at a church service with her family. I reassure her that I will take care of the family and I do. Christmas morning at 5:00 a.m. I help to deliver a chubby little boy to his ecstatic parents. Soon, their whole family comes over to welcome this little guy and again, I am humbled by how beautiful life can be. They name him Christopher. I can't think of a better way to spend Christmas morning. Meadow comes in around noon to take over and I go straight to my parent's house.

My parents have always had a live tree and this year is no different. My sister did most of the decorating so it is very colorful and chaotic. She found and put up all the old ornaments we made as children, egg crate angels, bedazzled cardboard snowflakes, and pipe cleaner candy canes. My family waited for me to open gifts, but I'm starving so we eat a lazy brunch first then relax together around the tree. I give my parents tickets to a Broadway show and a Sixers' game. They give me a robe and slippers and a full-day pass to a spa. They want me to take better care of myself. I give Janine an iPad. She cries and gives me a sweater with a matching scarf. We hug. She whispers in my ear.

"I have another gift for you but I have to give it to you later."

"OK." I say. I'm intrigued but exhausted, so I go upstairs to take a nap while they prepare for the rest of the family to arrive.

By 7:00 p.m., the house is packed with family. We have finished and cleaned up dinner. My cousin's three kids are running around with their new toys, my grandmother is commanding conversation from the easy chair in the living room, and my sister and her boyfriend are cuddling on the couch. *It's a Wonderful Life* is playing at my mom's annual insistence and she and I are watching it, drinking eggnog, and eating cookies. It's pretty much a perfect day and I am feeling blessed and happy.

After George Bailey finds out that he, indeed, is the richest man in town, tears still shining in our eyes, Janine turns to me and grins. I grin back at her. She disentangles herself from Joe and motions me upstairs. I follow her wondering what she is up to. We get up to my old room; she flicks on the light and plops on the bed. I sit down, ready for whatever talk we are going to have about her boyfriend. Instead, she leans down and pulls a red envelope from under the bed and hands it to me. It's addressed to me but at my parent's street address. I recognize the handwriting immediately. It's from Candace.

"It came a couple of days ago. I didn't want to give it to you right away because I wasn't sure what it would say and I didn't want it to ruin your holiday," she shrugs, then leans closer.

"But yesterday, I saw Candace's sister in the grocery store"....

"And?" I reply.

"Just open it!" she squeaks bouncing up and down.

I run my finger under the flap and tear the envelope open. It's a Christmas card with Rudolph on the front. I open it and below the usual holiday greetings is Candace's note to me:

Dee,

I hope you are having a wonderful holiday season. I'm in town for a while and I would love to see you. Please give me a call when you get a chance.

Love,

Candace

I turn the card over again and frown at it. I'm imagining her with her family around a Christmas tree. I put the card down on my lap.

"Hmm ... well, this was nice of her. So, she's in town for the holidays. Why are you so excited?"

"Yesterday, I was at the Rite-Aid getting tape when I saw Denise again. She was surprisingly cordial to me, maybe it was the holiday spirit, whatever, but I thought of you, of course, and I asked about Candace and her family. She said that Candace was in town but that her family didn't come with her. When I said, 'Oh, that's too bad, well, I guess she'll be going back for the New Year or something like that.' Denise said, 'I doubt it.' "Then she asked about you!!! Which she would never do, right? Because she hates you, right?"

I frown. "I guess she hates me, but what are you getting at, Janine?"

"Candace is back home and she didn't come with her family! It's the holidays?!?! Isn't that strange? Aren't you excited???"

I wasn't actually. I look at Janine and I look back down at the card trying to discern a hidden message and wondering what it means, if it means anything at all. Suddenly, I just feel tired. I look back up at Janine, who is lit up like a Christmas tree, and I smile at her. I lean to give her a big hug and I say "thank you." I'm thinking about what a great sister she is; she's convinced she has given me a gift of hope. She bounces out the room and back to Joe. I watch her go. It was a really great day. I'm not sure what this card means, but I guess I'll find out soon enough. But not today, today I just want another eggnog and some pound cake and to watch *The Preacher's Wife* with my mom.

Well, the next day I'm way too tired to call Candace. The day after that, I'm back to work and catching up with my co-workers and their holiday stories. The following day, I take a long run, pay my end of the year bills, donate to Alex's Lemonade Stand, and then I'm tired. The next day I admit to myself that I am avoiding making the call. I stand in front of the mirror and take a long look at myself. Yes, I have a slight holiday rounding but I'm OK with that — it's my winter insulation. Yes, I could get my ends cut and my hair oiled. I have a pang of regret that I cannot go back to Shari's salon. I look at myself and wonder at my hesitation. She's in town, she's probably leaving soon, she wants to say "hi", and didn't I call and say I wanted to be friends??? Janine has me anxious. I'm being ridiculous. I pick up the phone to call Viv, but the phone rings just as I swipe it on. It's Viv.

"Hey," I say, "I was just about to call you. Guess what?"

"Hey, Dee. Me first. I had a shitty Christmas. You want to come out here for New Year's? I don't think I can take another holiday alone. It was just ... so ... lonely. I have some miles. I'll buy your ticket, OK? But come. I need a friend. Please."

I have never heard Viv sound so sad. I don't think she has ever needed anybody for anything. The practice is not going to like it, but I have to go.

"OK. Buy the tickets – I have to be home on the 2nd though. They are going to fire me otherwise, OK?"

"Got it. I'll call you back with the details. Stay by your phone, I may need some info. Oh, what did you want to tell me?"

"Oh, nothing. We'll talk when I get there."

"OK, start packing. I'm getting the earliest flight I can get."

I call the job. I was right. Nobody is really happy about covering me again, but I make some trades and swaps – I'll be on weekend call for the next four months – and I work it all out. I pack though I honestly have no idea what it is like in California in the winter, nor do I know what we'll be doing. I pack the most neutral and flexible clothes I have that are clean with some fancy jewelry and hope for the best. Viv calls back in an hour and gives me the info for a red-eye. She was not playing, but I am ready. I think about calling Candace. I know I'm being a punk, but I just don't want to face another one of my failures. I can't take another disappointment. Some California sun is probably just what I need. And Viv.

❧ CHAPTER TWENTY-FOUR ❧

The red-eye to Los Angeles is a great flight for people watching, but I decide to tune out and read. I picked up a new Stephen King novel in the airport and unfortunately, it keeps me awake almost the whole flight. I am a weary and red-eyed mess by the time we land. Viv, dressed in army green cargo pants and a white linen button-down shirt, greets me with a cinnamon bun and a coffee and cannot stop laughing at me.

"I feel better already!" she says and gives me a big squeeze. We drive to her modest apartment off Moorpark Street. The building is a squat modern affair with a parking lot in the back. We are greeted by her tawny and vivacious Labradoodle, Butter. Apparently it's short for butterscotch, Butterfingers, Butterball, buttermilk, or any other number of butter words. She is adorable and friendly and clearly the apple of Viv's eye, if you judge by the size and amount of "her" personal affects all over the apartment. Trying not to trip over Butter, I take the obligatory tour, particularly enjoying the balcony, which looks out onto a beautiful flower-filled communal courtyard. Viv is talking about something as I sit at her kitchen table. She decides to make us brunch and starts clanging around. But I start nodding and taking pity on me, she directs me to the bedroom. The last thing I see is Butter's cute furry face up close to mine. She's sniffing at me curiously. I close my eyes and sleep.

Viv wakes me up around 2:00 p.m.

"Can't let you sleep too long or you'll never be right. I packed a picnic. Let's take a hike." A what? Since when do we hike? That's what I'm thinking, but I'm all disoriented and I just blink at her. "What?"

Wearing a pair of Viv's Timberlands (she has three pairs, don't ask why), we drive to Runyon Canyon. Of course, Butter has come with us and Viv is decked out with backpack, leash, poopy-scoop bags, a portable water bowl, snacks for us, a 2-liter water container, and a MediPack. I stand there gaping at her.

"Are you for real? Who are you and what have you done with Viv?"

"Just the Cali life, I guess. It's beautiful outside, so we hike and well, got to be prepared." She shrugs and pops out a walking stick from her trunk. I almost fall over laughing.

"What? It's gets tricky sometimes, and there are coyotes, so it's good to have a weapon just in case."

I hop right back into the car. I hold my ground for five minutes but you know, when in Rome.... And besides, it was a bright and sunny 65-degree day. Who could obsess about mortal danger on such a nice day?

It turns out to be a beautiful hike on a well-worn trail. We pass other hikers, many with dogs, some with kids, but the majority of people just by themselves, quiet and peaceful looking. We are quiet too, mostly just keeping an eye on Butter and enjoying the challenge of the sloping hill and the emerging view below us. It feels almost rude to talk surrounded by such natural beauty, but after a while my curiosity trumped nature's majesty.

"So, Viv. You sounded so upset on the phone. What happened at Christmas?"

She was quiet for a long time.

"Morgan has a new girlfriend. They're getting married this spring. I found out through a mutual friend of ours.

She let it slip on Christmas Eve. And so … a shitty Christmas."

"I'm so sorry, Viv."

"Yeah, I mean, it's over, it's been over, but still. Now it's really over and I … I hope I haven't made a mistake."

"Viv. You moved to a place that's always warm and sunny, you have a new job that you love, a cool apartment, and you have Butter, clearly the cutest dog in the world, and I don't even like dogs that much."

"Yup, you're right. I do like my life here. It's been good for me. I feel more calm but also, more alive. Could be all the outside air." She smiles and keeps walking.

"Still," she says, "it was a shitty Christmas." We walk up a steep incline. I'm starting to get winded.

"Are we going somewhere in particular?" I ask.

"Up."

I don't ask any more questions. I just follow her up the path and think. We come to a fork in the trail and Viv follows sharply to the left. In a few minutes, we come out to a small clearing. There is a bench overlooking a beautiful view of the city. Someone has placed a tiny statuette of the Buddha on a rocky cliff and people have built small rock sculptures around it. Further down the hill I can see where someone used pebbles to outline a heart in the dirt. We sit down and rest. Viv pours some water for Butter and hands me a bottle. I don't realize how thirsty I am until I take that first gulp.

"Easy, sis. You're going to want some of that later." I look over at Viv and she is rolling a joint. I can't remember the last time I smoked weed. I quickly go over my schedule and figure out I won't be back to work for four days. I can have a smoke. Viv lights it up, takes a toke and passes it to me. I inhale and immediately cough it all back up. My second attempt, I'm smarter and take a shallower hit. Nice. I sit back and feel the sun on my face.

"So how are you doing, Dee? Over Noema I hope. That bitch!" We laugh.

"Yeah, I guess. Mostly. It was messed up though, right?"

"Yeah, so now what? Anybody new yet?"

"No...but I did get a Christmas card from Candace." She glances over at me with a raised eyebrow. "And she was back in Philly...." She takes another toke and passes it to me. I take another small hit and give it back. "She wanted to meet me."

"Ahhh ... here we come to it. So what happened?" She licks her fingers and pinches out the joint. I wince for her.

"Nothing happened. I never called her." Silence. "She's back with her husband and I don't think I can be just friends with her. When I saw her in Santa Fe it just all came back and oh, Viv. Remember how I loved her?" I'm feeling much more relaxed now.

"Yeah, I remember. You two were good together. I was jealous." I look at her.

"No, silly, I didn't want you or her, but I was jealous of what you had. It was so intense and so real and so grown-up. And you were so happy, like all the time."

"I was, wasn't I?" I smile up at the sun.

"Look, I'm going to take Butter up to this spot where she likes to do her business. You wait here. You look peaceful. Why don't you pray to Buddha and see if you get enlightened."

"I'm pretty sure that's not the way it works, Viv."

"Whatever, Dee, just enjoy the vibe. I'll be about 10 to fifteen minutes." Viv untangles Butter's leash and they exit out to a tiny trail just behind us. I listen to the wind. I can just make out the distant voices of other hikers. Somewhere, someone is singing. I study the face on the Buddha – the epitome of calm. I luxuriate in my first high in like 10 years and I think about Candace and me.

We had been good together. I try to think about all the women since Candace. The flings in college and grad school, the semi-serious girlfriends in Philly, Pepper, Noema. I can see all their faces. I can remember most of their names, but love? Did I love any of them? Yes, one or two. Did any of them love me? Maybe, but how can I be sure? What do I know about love anyway? How did I get to be 32 years old and am still so unsure about what the hell I am doing or how to love? The only love I was ever sure about was Candace and I totally ruined it.

I sit up and replay that thought. The only love I was ever sure about was Candace and I totally ruined it. After that … after I messed that up so badly, I was just lost. I lost trust. I lost confidence. I lost innocence. I lost love. I lost me, me at my best. The thought makes me groan out loud but it resonates and repeats and echoes around in my head and I know it for truth.

I hear Viv coming back through the trees, but I see Butter first. She bounds to me, giddily off the leash and jumps up on my lap. I rub her head and body. She's so purely and completely happy, it brings tears to my eyes. Not a care in the world, that dog. Lucky dog.

We hike back down the canyon, careful of stumps and stones and rattlesnakes. We pass by people going up. I wonder if we look calm and peaceful to them. At first, I still feel the heavy airiness of the high but as we descend, I leave it behind bit by bit. What remains is the unnerving awareness that I am not whole. And I can't un-see the gap, the chasm left in the bright, young wonderful creature that was me before I lost her.

❧ CHAPTER TWENTY-FIVE ❧

The next day is New Year's Eve and Viv takes me "sightseeing". First we go by her office, then to the car wash, then we walk Butter, then to Whole Foods and finally, thankfully, to In-And-Out Burger because I am starving! After I beg for some real LA culture, we finally walk down Sunset, but by then I am tired and need a nap if I'm ever going to be able to stay up for midnight. I think we drive past Drew Barrymore on our way back to her house but I can't be sure. I squeal anyway. Viv laughs at me, of course, but I don't care, I love Drew Barrymore!

We get back to her place by 7:00 p.m. We have a glass of wine and I lay down for a nap. Butter joins me. When Viv wakes me at 9:00 p.m., I'm ready to go but she looks tired.

"Did you sleep?" I ask her. She sits on the bed next to me.

"No." She hesitates. "I called Morgan." I can only just shake my head.

"I hope you didn't do or say anything stupid," I say, sitting up and regretting my nap.

"No. I just wanted it to be cool between us. I wanted her to know that I know and that I just want her to be happy. Even if I'm not quite there." She looks sad but smiles at me. I lean over and hug her. She tries to pull away but I hold on.

"Viv, that was a very mature thing to do. I am utterly shocked." She laughs but I don't let go.

"I know you miss her, but you were right. I think this is the place for you and you deserve to be fully happy. Even if you're not today, you will be. I know it. I feel it."

"Thanks, Dee," she sniffs.

I can feel my shoulder wet with her tears, but when she pulls away again, I let her.

She sits back and looks at me.

"You're a good friend, Dee. I'm so glad we're back in touch. I didn't know how much I missed your friendship."

"I feel the same way, Viv. Good friends are hard to find. Now, come on. We have to get ready to go. You promised me that we would be out having fun for the New Year and I intend to do just that. Let's go."

Viv walked over to the stereo, put on some Grand Central Funk, and we showered and dressed. Of course, she ended up 10 times more glamorous than I could ever aspire to. She wore a cream-colored suit with a sheer white blouse underneath. The shirt itself plunged down to her navel while the rest of the suit was fairly conservative. She even wore a pocket square. It was fine lesbian gear – sexy and strong, but expensive. I decided to play on my strengths and went with Afro-funk goddess. I picked my hair out, slithered into tight black jeans and a black leather vest, threw on my chunkiest, most fabulous African-inspired jewelry with the deepest red lipstick I own. I snapped in some vintage butterfly hair clips to give my hair some retro funk. We looked good. Very different, but good, really good.

When we pull up to The Abbey, there is a line around the block of the most beautiful people I have ever seen.

Despite my own fabulousness, I am humbled. LA is some whole other shit. I groan at the line and Viv just laughs. We valet park a block down on Santa Monica, but the walk back is relaxing. The air is cool, but there is balminess that keeps it from being chilled. As we get to the line, Viv walks right past it. I rush to follow her and ask her where she's going.

She looks at me, makes to clutch her pearls, and says with great indignation, "Dee, I thought you knew me. I wouldn't make you fly all the way here and not have VIP passes. Chile, please."

She shakes her head, links her arm with mine and we stroll up to the other side of the gated patio entrance. She presents our passes to the most beautiful bodyguard I have ever seen. Tall, built, and beautiful like Laila Ali, but I'm pretty sure she could kick our asses in three seconds flat, just like Laila Ali. Luckily, she just nods at us and I take a deep breath as we go in.

The place is huge and full of glitter. No, really. The dancers up on the bars are literally tossing handfuls of glitter onto dancers on the floor. They twirl around in it like figures in a snow globe. The place is beautiful with gleaming dark wood floors, vaulted beamed ceilings, and rough brick walls contrasting with the slate patio entrance. But it's the people that really dazzle. I remind myself that aspiring actors and models come out to Hollywood to become stars. These aren't normal people.

Viv looks around then smiles at me. We head to the closest bar. She orders us two Black Lilies. I raise my eyebrow at her, but when the drinks come 15 minutes later and I take my first sip, I understand. That is one spicy little number and it melted away any nerves I may have had. We take a quick selfie. Well, we take a few until we get a perfect one, and then we slowly make our way around the different levels of the club. Viv introduces me to a few people she knows, but mostly we just people-watch and scope out the women. As two of the few African-American women there, we get noticed and a few women catch my attention. But honestly, these are not my people and I think I'd rather just dance with the boys.

I set down my empty glass and head onto the dance floor. Viv follows me and we jam to re-mixed Madonna classics. I lose myself in the lights and music, but wave to her when she heads off the floor. I dance with a sexy young boy for a few, then turn to find a short brunette all over me. I give her my best fever and then turn to give it to a blonde with a pixie cut. I take in the joy all around me and revel in not knowing a soul.

The DJ announces that it is five minutes to the New Year and the bars load up with glasses of champagne. I step off the floor to grab one as I look around for Viv. I finally find her on the dance floor with a curvy and very pretty Latina woman. I love watching Viv dance. She is sheer sophisticated raunchiness. I make my way over to them. The DJ lowers the music and starts the countdown.

"15, 14, 13…."

Viv points to her friend and yells, "Dee, this is Alana, Alana, this is my best friend, Dee." We smile and wave "hello" and we all join in the countdown. "…. 4, 3, 2, 1!"

I sip my champagne, Viv kisses her new friend, and the whole club erupts in celebration. I get sloshed with champagne; Viv grabs mine and finishes it off then gives me a big bear hug. "I love you, Celie!" I laugh and laugh. I haven't felt this good in a while. The DJ somehow mixes Kool and the Gang's "Celebration" with "Turn Down for What" and the whole club piles onto the floor. We dance ourselves into a frenzy.

I finally need a rest and start off the dance floor when I feel my purse vibrate. I back into a corner and check my phone. I have a text from my sister. It says, "Happy New Year to the best sister a girl ever had! I hope you and Viv are having fun." She attached a picture of her and Joe wearing party hats and blowing noisemakers. I smile and quickly send the picture of Viv and me with a similar message.

After I close the app, I glance at my Facebook icon. I see a few notifications. I glance up at Viv, but she is busy at the bar talking to Alana. I hate to be "that" girl at the club all in her phone, but I pull up my Facebook anyway. I have a message from Candace. It's a friend request. I confirm it and go to her page. Her profile picture takes my breath away. It's just a close-up of her, but somehow my heart still skips a beat.

I write a quick message on her wall. "Happy New Year to you and your family, Candace. Sorry I missed you in Philly, maybe next year?" I glance at her picture again and am about to close the app and put my phone away when I see a message pop up. It's her. "Hi Dee, Happy New Year to you, too but it's just me now. Thought about you a lot tonight, like every New Year's Eve. Probably shouldn't say that. Sorry. Wine ..."

A current goes through me. I pause and read back through her message. "What do you mean, just you?"

She responds, "That's what I wanted to talk to you about in Philly." My heart starts racing and I don't know why. I mean, I know why but ... slow down ... slow down. Take a breath, Dee.

I look at Viv. She is laughing and flirting with Alana. She notices me and smiles. She mouths, "You OK?" I nod yes and wave her back to her conversation. I stare at my phone and bite my lip.

I type, "Oh." She replies, "Where are you?" I respond, "I'm in LA with Viv. Where are you?" She writes, "Albuquerque. I got in this morning." I type back, "Can I come see you?" A pause, then she responds, "Yes!" I type, "I'll be there tomorrow. Sweet dreams." I close the app and put my phone away.

Feeling anxious and excited, I look for Viv but she is back on the dance floor with Alana. I head out to join them and I can't stop smiling. My phone vibrates and I look down at a picture of a smiling Candace raising a glass of wine to me. Viv sees the picture and says, "What???" But I yell, "I'll tell you about it later. Your friend wants to dance." I spin her around to Alana and make eye contact with an unattached beauty. The DJ puts on "It's Time for the Percolator", and the whole club loses its collective mind. I dance my happiness into the universe.

❧ CHAPTER TWENTY-SIX ❧

On New Year's Day, I manage to get a 3:00 p.m. flight to Albuquerque by going stand-by. Viv was not at all mad that I cut our visit short. I actually think she was more excited than me when I showed her the messages. And I think she may have already made a date with Alana for that night. Viv is not one to be patient. The flight is short but sweet. I vacillate between being excited and hopeful to being cautious and practical. I try to nap, but that is a lost cause and not even Steven King can distract me. My stomach has butterflies and I fight to keep my composure.

When I finally get to baggage claim, I am tired. I step out of the airport to look for a taxi and am again enthralled by the sky. The sun is setting and the contrast of the glowing orange clouds against the clear azure sky above makes me want to weep. The arrival of a cab interrupts my reverie but the driver understands. He gets out to gaze as well. I can hear him sigh. A minute later, we look at each other and smile.

"That's why I moved out here, young lady. Now, can I help you with your bags?"

I nod. His gentle, pleasant conversation is just what I need for the drive to Candace's house. On the way, I text her that I will be there in a few minutes. She just sends an emoji with big wide eyes. I laugh. The driver drops me off at her house and I tip him well. Her block is weirdly quiet until I remember that it's New Year's Day and most people are recovering from something.

I walk up her steps, familiar and unfamiliar to me now, and I ring the bell. She answers the door in a simple but becoming yellow wrap dress. A matching scarf that drapes over her shoulder ties her hair back. She looks beautiful, but I try not to notice much. She moves back to let me in and I feel self-conscious about my bags. I lug them in and try to set them down gracefully and out of the way.

"Happy New Year," I say.

"Happy New Year, Dee" she replies.

She closes the door behind us and we embrace. I inhale. She smells sweet and spicy, like ginger. When I open my eyes, I can see her dining table is set for dinner. There are flowers and candles and wine glasses. She grins at me and my stomach starts rumbling.

"So, you can you cook?" I laugh.

She looks insulted. "Of course, I can cook! My mama didn't raise three girls and not teach us how to cook. Come on. I'll show you." She takes my hand and walks me to the table. Black-eyed peas with turkey legs, collard greens, candied yams, corn bread, and tamales are all laid out in matching dishes.

"It's ready. Would you like some wine?" she asks.

"Oh God, yes I would. Thanks."

I take a seat while she pours and serves us both. She says the grace and we begin to eat. The food is delicious, but after a minute I put down my fork and look at her.

"Am I really here? I feel like this is a dream or I'm on some kind of trip. You know, Viv gave me weed. I just…this is crazy. I can't believe I'm here and you're here." I shake my head.

"OK, tell me what happened," I say.

She sits back and looks at me.

"OK," she replies. She takes a deep breath then just blurts it out all in a rush, "Ramon and I did not work out. We went to couples therapy and we ended up talking about you and our relationship in high school and when I told him you had come out to visit ..."

She pauses and shakes her head.

"He couldn't really forgive me for cheating on him and he just couldn't get past my past with you. And I ... I tried but I couldn't stop thinking about you, either." She paused, thinking. "And I was honest about that. But I wanted to stay anyway, for the kids, but he was angry at me and they could see that and it just wasn't going to work. So he left and took the kids with him."

"I'm really sorry," I say, waiting. She takes another big breath and continues.

"So, I went home at Christmas to tell my family about that...and to tell them that I am gay."

"Oh!" is all that I can manage.

"For years, no, for my whole life, I have done what they wanted. I have tried to live up to their expectations, but where has that gotten me? I moved to New Mexico to get away from them so I could be my own person, but I'm not, I wasn't. I was still living by my mother's rules, still doing what she says. I'm a grown woman. Why am I still trying to live my life to please my mother?" she asks.

I shake my head and hold my tongue.

"I mean seriously, Dee. When I was out to dinner with you, I felt like that was where I was supposed to be. I didn't feel weird or awkward. Nobody pointed fingers at us or even paid any attention to us. Why should I be miserable because my mother might be embarrassed at church? She should love me no matter what. And if she has a problem, that's just it, that's her problem. I am choosing to be free, I am choosing to be happy," she declares. She could not be more beautiful in her determination. I am trying not to notice.

I am speechless, but I have tears in my eyes. I know what a big step this is for her, for anybody, and I am happy for her. I am trying to remain neutral, to not think ahead, to not guess or imagine or hope. I want to be supportive. I want to be a good friend. I nod. I smile. I close my eyes and try to shake off hope.

"When the therapist made me talk about you, it took me back to who I was back then. When I was your girlfriend, I felt like I could do and be anything. I felt like I was truly myself."

"I recently had the exact same thought, but I thought it might be, you know, the weed or something," I say. We laugh.

"We were good together, Candace. I'm really, so, so very sorry that I ruined that. I was young and immature and it was all so new and so perfect and I was just so jealous…"

"Stop, Dee. I know you are sorry and so am I, but that was the past. I have forgiven you for that. And I don't want you to carry that anymore, OK? Can you forgive yourself for it?"

I take a minute and really think about it. I think of myself at seventeen. I was gawky and smart, strong-willed, and filled with big plans for the future. I always liked that girl. She just made a mistake, a big ole passion-filled mistake. I smile at that. "Yeah," I say, "I can forgive her, and I do. She was just a kid. *I* was just a kid."

"Yeah," she says. "We were just kids but I have a question for you, the grown-up Dee."

"Yes?" I say in my most grown up and sultry voice.

"Are you seeing anybody right now?" she asks.

I shake my head and say, "No, ma'am."

"Would you like to go on a date with me?" she asks.

I want to say something like 'maybe we should wait, you're new to all this, you're just getting out of a marriage' but instead I say, "Yes." I'm suddenly choked with emotion.

"I don't know how this would work, but I know my heart still beats for you. I don't know how or why but when I saw you, when I kissed you, I knew I was still in love with you. It doesn't even seem possible after all these years…but I do love you, still."

I look at her and shake my head. I feel utterly amazed.

She takes my hands in hers and leans forward to kiss my tear. It feels like a blessing. I open my eyes and laugh. She laughs too. I lift my head and kiss her lips. They are soft and sweet and full of the love and passion I remember.

"Candace, I know we have a lot of things to figure out, but I just want to enjoy this. This day, your face, this relief I feel. I know I went looking for you, but somehow I feel like you found me!"

"Sorry it took me so long." She looks genuinely remorseful.

"It's OK. I think I'm finally ready to be found."

I catch my breath and smile at her smiling at me. I'm nervous but excited all the same. I feel happy, hopeful … and whole.

"Try the black-eyed peas, Dee, before they get cold. That's my signature dish."

I turn back to my dinner and still smiling, I begin to eat. It's delicious. I look up to tell her so but her gaze silences me. I remember that look. She still loves me. After all this time, she still loves me. I close my eyes for a moment and offer up thanks. When I open them, I begin my life again, with Candace.

ACKNOWLEDGEMENTS

Special thanks to my fellow creative sisters; Angelou Deign, Yvonne Jones, Aishah Shahidah Simmons, Kelly Ward, Roxana Walker-Canton, and Julie Yarbrough, who took the time to read my manuscript and give me honest feedback. But most of all, thanks for the wonderful support and encouragement. I especially want to express my gratitude to Yvonne Jones, who guided me through this maze of self-publishing, and availed me of her editing expertise. I also want to thank Marva Smith for her excellent copyediting and wonderful words of wisdom. I would also like to thank Melicia Escobar, CNM who helped me keep my midwifery within the realm of reality, though I still took some liberties. Finally, I would be remiss if I did not acknowledge two excellent women who have passed on but whose friendship, generosity of spirit and unfailing support still inspire me, Leslie Esdaile Banks and Sharon Campbell Evans.